BRAND OF THE HUNTED

T
bu
it
pa
th
hu
th
T
th
th
ta
m
la

BRAND OF THE HUNTED

by

Charles M. Barker

Dales Large Print Books
Long Preston, North Yorkshire,
BD23 4ND, England.

British Library Cataloguing in Publication Data.

Barker, Charles M.
    Brand of the hunted.

A catalogue record of this book is
available from the British Library

    ISBN   1-84262-288-9 pbk

First published in Great Britain 1963
Originally published in paperback as *Brand of the Hunted* by
Chuck Adams
First Hardcover edition 2003 by Robert Hale Ltd.

Copyright © 1963, 2003 John Glasby

Cover illustration © Faba by arrangement with
Norma Editorial S.A.

Published in Large Print 2004 by arrangement with
Robert Hale Ltd.

Dales Large Print is an imprint of Library Magna Books Ltd.

Printed and bound in Great Britain by
T.J. (International) Ltd., Cornwall, PL28 8RW

1

Riding the Wide Range

At first the trail to the east had been deserted, empty as far as the eye could see, but now there was a small, scarcely seen cloud of dust in the far distance where it came in out of the mountains, to cross the wide, stretching wilderness of the dusty plain.

Neil Roberts sat easily in the saddle, hands resting loosely on the pommel, eyes narrowed a little against the glare of the sun now climbing up swiftly from the eastern horizon, red turning yellow, soon to become white as it approached the zenith, when the waves of heat would lift over the range and the dust-devils would cavort and whirl madly around the buttes.

He was a limber man with a rider's looseness about him, about every move of his tall, lean body the grey eyes half-hidden beneath the lowered lids, the crinkly hair just showing beneath the wide-brimmed hat that kept some of the sunlight off his face. All of his features were angular and solid, and his shape was lean and stringy, the shape of a man who lived in the saddle, whose home was the great rolling distances of the prairie and whose ceiling was the sky.

The rising whorls of dust, perhaps ten, maybe fifteen miles away, drew closer, the only evidence that whatever it was out there was moving. But as they drew closer, it was possible to make out some form of shape in the grey dust.

The tiny dots, barely seen at first, drew themselves out from the shimmering heat waves, moving slowly in single file, big wagons each drawn by four powerful horses.

From that distance, it was impossible to make out how many there were in the train, but he guessed there must have been close on sixteen or twenty of them, heading west along the trails which cut through almost a dozen states, through some of the roughest and most dangerous country in the world; not only dangerous because of the miles of arid, alkali desert, high mountains that had to be crossed, great rivers in full flood; but because of the other dangers which lay hidden in that country. Men who would stop at nothing to destroy the wagon trains, the big cattle bosses whose cattle roamed the wild wilderness of the prairie, and then the border gangs, the men who lived off the wagon trains, murdering and plundering.

And at the end of the trail, for the fortunate few who made it, the Promised Land – California, a land so they said flowing in milk and honey, where gold nuggets as big as a man's fist were to be had for the taking, and where the soil and climate were so good that whole cities were springing up virtually overnight as people moved in from the east.

He forced a quick grin. He was a man who could grin whenever the going became tough, whose smile was inclined to touch not only his mouth but his eyes too. Yet he was also a brooding man with something that often showed at the back of the cold, grey eyes; as if a hidden devil lay somewhere in their depths from which it would sometimes leap up unbidden, naked and threatening, only to sink down again behind the veiling lids.

A quick glance at the sun told him that the wagon train would not reach him much before early afternoon, even if they pushed their horses to the limit, which did not seem likely.

He put his mount down the gentle slope

towards the bank of the river, where there was shade from the tall trees that grew along the water's edge. Alighting, he lay flat on his belly upstream from his horse and drank deeply of the cool water, then filled his canteen, an action born of long years in the desert when each drop of water was a precious thing.

Going back towards the trees, he seated himself in the shade of the tallest, resting his back and shoulders against the broad trunk. In the distance, his mount moved lazily along the river bank, drifting to graze. He pulled his hat down over his eyes, stretching his lean body out.

He woke when the heat of the sun shone full on to his face again, sat upright, looking about him, knowing that he had been asleep for some hours. The sorrel was still there, twenty yards away, grazing peacefully and, in the distance, the dull cloud that almost shrouded the wagon train was now less than a couple of miles away. He could just make out the faint calls of the drivers and the outriders as they urged their flagging horses forward to the river.

Back to the east there lay only desert for more than fifty miles and Neil knew that the horses in the train, and the cows they were bringing too, would have smelled the water by now, would be straining at the traces.

Standing up, he whistled to his mount, swung himself up into the saddle, then put the horse into the water. In the middle of the river, where the current flowed strongest, he could feel it push against the horse's chest as it breasted the current, at times forced to swim across.

On the other side, he rode towards the lead wagon, giving the sorrel its head. Down a slight slope he went, reining as he came alongside the wagon, staring up at the barrel-chested man who rode it, sitting easily on the lip of the seat. A big man of sinew and muscle and bone, with flaming red hair and a beard to match, reddish and ragged. The floppy, wide-brimmed hat was pulled down well over his forehead, but sweat ran in rivulets down his face and the white alkali dust, burning and stinging, had worked its way into the folds of his skin, mingling with the perspiration until it formed a streaky mask from which his eyes peered out, black and piercing under the thick, tufted brows. There was a rifle, a Winchester, Neil noticed, thrust into a leather scabbard on the side of the wagon within easy reach of his huge hands.

'Clem Jackson?' Neil called, as he turned

the sorrel, riding alongside the other, his mount easily matching pace with the wagon.

'That's my name,' growled the other in a deep voice that seemed to come booming all the way from the lowermost depths of his chest.

'Mine's Neil Roberts. Perhaps Weston mentioned my name before you left.'

'Roberts.' The other nodded slowly, ponderously. 'We were warned to keep a look out for you, didn't expect to run into you so soon.'

'I figured you might run into trouble around this neck of the territory and came along as fast as I could. There's bad country ahead.'

'Figgered that might be so.' The other's glance strayed towards the Winchester. 'Didn't intend taking any chances. We've put all we got into these wagons, and we don't aim to let anybody take them away from us without a fight. We're headed for California and, by God, that's where we're going.'

'I'm sure you'll make it, but it won't be easy. In the meantime, you've probably noticed there's a river dead ahead, less than a mile further on. You could make camp there, plenty of water for your horses and cattle, and I could have a pow-wow with you. There's a lot of things I ain't got quite straight in my mind yet, and if I'm in to take this train through the country up ahead, I'd like the answers to some questions.'

For a moment he saw the hesitation in the other, then the huge frame relaxed and the man grinned.

'I like you, Roberts,' he growled. 'You're the kind of man I could trust. They told me that much when we started out, but I never take a man on trust, no more'n I'd take a horse or a wagon. I like to look them over first and make up my own mind.'

He flicked the bull-hide whip over the horses, urging them on, but by now the animals had got the scent of water and needed no urging. The Conestoga wagons rumbled forward, wheels creaking on their axles as they bumped and swayed over the rough, uneven ground. Up ahead the water shone and glistened in the bright, harsh sunlight and the whooping of the men riding scout told that they had already reached it.

Half an hour later the wagons had been drawn up in a wide circle on the eastern bank of the river. They would not ford it until the horses had been watered and everything had been checked. The river was deep in the middle and the current strong.

Seated opposite Clem Jackson, Neil ate the beans and bacon which had been handed him on a plate slowly, chewing easily on the appetising food. He had lived for so long on jerked beef, eaten cold, washed down with water, that this food, and the hot coffee that went with it, filled his stomach well.

'You reckon's there's a chance of getting through along this trail, Roberts?' asked Jackson suddenly. He glanced up and eyed Neil shrewdly with his dark, brooding eyes. 'They warned us that it wouldn't be easy this way, that we ought to have taken the northern trail. But that would have added a hundred days to the journey, and it's bad country there, especially if we're caught in the winter.'

'That's right.' Neil nodded in agreement. 'But I ought to warn you of what lies ahead of you if you still want to take this trail.'

He waved a hand almost negligently towards the east, back along the trail they had just come. There was a grim trace of amusement in his tone as he said:

'Back there you drove these wagons across more than fifty miles of alkali desert, and most of you probably figgered that if you could do that, you could do anything. But that was nothing compared with what lies in that direction.' He jerked a thumb to the west.

'Doesn't look too bad to me once we ford the river,' muttered a short, dark-haired man.

'Maybe not. But it ain't the country you'll have to fight there. Plenty of water between the big rivers, plenty of grazing, too. And plenty of trouble. Mebbe you never heard of the Shermans and the Hollards.'

'Nope, can't say I have,' went on the other with unconscious arrogance.

His words sounded too sharp and distinct, the tone just a mite too clear for Neil's liking. But he kept his temper, knowing that a Western man had a looser and easier way of speaking. He guessed this man came from way back east, maybe thought he knew everything there was to know about the west and wasn't inclined to accept advice.

Neil smiled in a wintry way, eyes deliberately as bleak as his voice.

'This is cattle country, mister. Stretching for the next three hundred miles to the west and more than twice that distance to the south and north, is all cattle land. Probably a hundred thousand head of prime beef cattle, all belonging to one of two men – Jesse Sherman or Matt Hollard. They don't like nesters, or even men like yourselves just passing through. This is their land, even though you might say that it was got illegally. But they hold it by force of arms, they have got their own bands of outlaws, hired gunmen whose job it is to shoot down anybody trespassing here and stop anybody like you from moving through.'

He grinned faintly.

'I suppose it's true to say that most of the time they're at each other's throats, rustling and killing. But they'll band together to fight any wagon train that tries to make its way across their land.'

'Then we'll fight,' grunted Jackson.

He reached out, picked up the long-barrelled Winchester holding it tightly in his hairy fists, the knuckles of his hands showing through the skin, glistening in white bone with the pressure he was exerting.

'Do you think that you can fight those men, professional fighting men, the scum of a hundred towns, men wanted by the law from here to the Mexican border, but safe so long as they work for these men?' He shook his head very slowly.

'Are you suggesting that we turn back, or maybe that we try to go around them?' asked Jackson tightly. He met Neil's steady glance with a brief show of impatience.

'If you don't want to turn back – and I figger that ain't likely seeing that you've come so far – then we'll have to go straight ahead. No point in trying to drive this wagon train around that territory. It would take the best part of seventy days to do it, and there's no guarantee you'd be safe even then.'

'So we drive straight on,' growled the big man.

Very slowly he relaxed his grip on the rifle, let it fall to the soft earth beside him. He picked up his mug of hot coffee, tilted it savagely to his lips and drank deeply of it, some of the scalding liquid splashing over his arms and bare chest, but he did not seem to notice it.

'Just so long as everybody in the train knows what they're letting themselves in for,' said Neil quietly, and evenly.

'They knew the danger before they agreed to join the train,' muttered Jackson thickly. 'They all agreed to come along and they elected me to be wagon master. They take their orders from me now. That's the way it's got to be.'

'Can you speak for all of them?' Neil glanced at him in surprise.

'That I can.' He nodded his head ponderously. 'And I say that we drive straight across this territory, and to hell with the Shermans and the Hollards, and their hired gunmen.'

Neil shrugged negligently.

'Very well.' He drained his coffee. 'If that's the way you want it. Better rest up your horses for the rest of the day out here. We can ford the river first thing tomorrow morning.'

'That makes sense,' agreed the dark-haired man. 'Ain't no sense in putting tired horses into that current.' He threw a quick glance at the sky, clear and cloudless. 'Weather's going to stay fine. Ain't likely to get swollen in the next few hours.'

The big man paused, then nodded, got heavily to his feet and went over to sit on the wagon tongue.

In the heat head of the afternoon, a deep and clinging silence lay over the camp. It was possible to make out the gurgling of the water over the smooth stones near the bank where the river ran faster. Lowering very slowly to the west, the prairie sun threw down the heat that was reflected from the desert in dizzying waves.

Men and women forsook the open for the shade inside the wagons, but even here there was a deep and sullen heat, nowhere was it possible to escape from it. It was something that had been their constant companion since they had entered the desert to the east some four days earlier.

Not until an hour before sundown did the heat pressure ease. Then the wind came sighing in from the north-west, blowing off the tall hills in the distance where they stood out on the skyline, a cooling wind that brought the men and women out of the wagons, around the fires which had been lit in the open.

Down by the river's edge Neil Roberts washed some of the dust from his face and neck, feeling the cold water sting his skin where it had been burned by the sun, rubbed raw by the alkali dust.

Around the fires they were cooking bacon, boiling coffee in the big pans, ladling it out into mugs, the smell of the steaming liquid lying over everything.

Neil pulled the lashing of his jacket tighter about him to keep out the cold night air. He rubbed a broad thumb against the butt of the Colt at his waist, stared across through the leaping flames at the leader of the wagon train.

'You said you had some questions you wanted to ask, Roberts,' boomed Jackson loudly. 'Go ahead. Ask them. I'll tell you all I can.'

'There's not much.' Neil shrugged, chewed reflectively on a strip of bacon. 'I know where you're headed – California. But why do you want me to lead you?'

'You're a fast man with a gun,' said the other bluntly. 'They told us that if necessary you shot first and talked later. You're the kind of man we need on this journey if they spoke the truth. Some of the dangers you've told us of, but there are bound to be others. We've heard something of what happened to the other trains that tried to get through. Some of 'em didn't even get as far as this. We passed some on the way here, back there in the alkali.'

Neil nodded, narrowing his eyes a little. For a moment he wasn't listening to the big man seated on the opposite side of the fire, and his eyes were fixed eastward on the flat, rolling face of the desert where the whiteness of the alkali seemed to shine eerily in the fading light of evening. He, too, had seen the remains of the small wagon trains that had tried to push their way westward and had met their fate out there in the terrible, heat-wavering wilderness where the days were scorched slices of hell, and the nights, long hours torn out of the arctic cold. The small trains, perhaps half a dozen wagons, had tried to cross without sufficient water, possibly without any real idea of what they were facing, of the only way to go; and they had died. Months later men had come across the remnants of the wagons, with the bleached bones lying beside them, all that was left of men and animals.

Now, any wagon trains heading west were larger, more than a score of wagons, plenty of water in the barrels they carried, all of the men armed with the latest weapons, repeating Winchesters, Colts, ready to meet trouble along the way.

'You can consider yourselves lucky if you've managed to get this far without trouble,' he said flatly. 'The going isn't likely to be as easy from now on.'

'We're ready to meet anybody who tries to stop us,' said the big man quietly. 'If we have to fight these hired killers you speak of, then we'll fight them. We're not looking for trouble, but if it comes...'

He left the rest of his sentence unsaid, but there was a tightening in his tone, a hard, grim determination.

'It will come, take my word for it.'

Neil glanced at the man beside him, then beyond the men at the fire towards the women and children clustered around the wagons drawn up around the fire. Perhaps the men were ready to fight it out with hired killers and the border gangs, he thought tightly, but what about them? His grey eyes were cold as he allowed his gaze to wander around the camp.

Night closed in swiftly from the east. For a brief moment the setting sun, hidden behind the mountains, touched the crests with a flash of red light as if a fire had been lit at the rear of the world. Then the darkness swamped it out and the stars were clear and crisp in the heavens overhead.

The horses settled down for the night, the handful of cattle they had brought with them lowed softly for a little while, then they too became silent. But the fires still burned among the wagons. Several of the men were still awake and guards had been posted.

Lying in his blanket, Neil listened to them, talking softly among themselves, as the long dark hours passed slowly, and the brilliant stars counted out the minutes in their slow wheel across the vast span of the heavens.

As he lay there he tried to think ahead, to assess the dangers which he knew would be lying in wait for them. For the next two hundred miles or so he could foresee the danger, but being able to foresee it did not necessarily mean that they would be able to overcome it.

The country to the west, whether it belonged to Sherman or Hollard, had a reputation for sheltering wild ones. Men quick with a gun, men who would shoot to kill on the slightest excuse. A wagon train such as this would be regarded as easy picking to them.

At the prospect of this he felt his skin tingling, prickling with a faintly uneasy apprehension. Once, in the red firelight, he turned to study the tall, big figure of the man who stood for almost an hour on the edge of the camp staring out towards the west, out across the wide river which they would ford in the morning at first light, and if there were any doubts in Jackson's mind about the outcome of the drive that stretched in front of them, none of them showed on his face. He seemed confident that they would win through, even though he probably accepted the fact that some of them in the train would inevitably die.

There was no movement by the big man as he stood on the edge of camp. He seemed utterly absorbed by what he was seeing in his mind's eye, out there beyond the stretch of the river. Neil drew a deep breath, pulled his blanket more tightly around his shoulders. The fire was dying a little now, the cold of the night creeping into his bones. Except for the guards, the wagon train slept.

The next morning, after eating breakfast over the rekindled fires, they began the crossing of the wide river, putting the horses into the water even before the sun had lifted clear of the eastern horizon.

Evenly balanced in the saddle, Neil sat and watched the lumbering wagons through narrowed eyes, alert for trouble. This was always a dangerous moment as far as a wagon train was concerned. Few of the men on the tongues of the great covered wagons were experts, and in the middle of the river the water was deep, the bottom difficult and treacherous, although fortunately the current was slow. It was hard driving, arms straining on the lashings and reins as the water breasted against the horses in a curling whiteness of foam and their feet slipped on the sandy bottom.

A dark-haired man dressed in leather yelled a sharp order as the water came over the tongue of the wagon on which he sat, the horses surged forward, thrusting against the river. Sam Jessup, Neil remembered the dark man's name from the previous evening when he had sat with the others around the blazing fire, listened to their talk, their hopes, their fears, their confidence that they would eventually win through to the rich yellow land of Southern California.

'Keep them moving!' Neil called to the rest of the men as the wagons rumbled ponderously into the river, began the long pull across to the further bank. He knew with a sure instinct that if one wagon faltered here, it could mean they would lose it in the mud.

There was another man, short and inclined to fatness, driving Jackson's wagon now, and the big wagon master was riding a high-spirited horse, urging the lumbering wagons forward, his loud, booming voice bellowing even above the rumble of the wheels on the dust of the trail. He turned in his saddle, came riding over towards Neil, his face expressionless.

'Once we cross the river, it ought to be good driving country,' he observed, nodding his shaggy head in the direction of the flat, rolling ground that lay on the other side of the river.

Neil nodded speculatively, remained silent, his face tight.

'You still worrying about those cattle men

who'll try to stop us?' growled the other harshly.

'I am. We won't see them, not at first. But they'll see us. It'd be impossible not to spot a wagon train this size. They'll try to kill us before we've gone a score of miles.'

The last of the wagons crossed the river, the horses straining in the traces as they hauled it up the far bank. Neil and Jackson waited until it was safely over, then put their mounts to the water, took them across.

The train had formed up, was moving slowly across the smooth stretch of country leading towards the rising curve of a low hill. There was no sign of a trail here, no place where the ground had been beaten flat by the pounding of countless hooves over the earth.

Around them everything lay quiet and still, with a watchful, waiting quality hanging over it, and Neil felt the muscles of his chest tighten a little in response to the silence. He thought without pleasure of what lay ahead of them, knew the hundred different kinds of danger and death which faced them here in this wild country, and more especially in the Badlands that lay further to the west.

But before they reached that terrible terrain they had first to make their way over the vast stretch of prairie. He threw a wide, sweeping glance around him, eyes narrowed a little against the vivid red glare of the rising sun, alert and watchful for the first signs of trouble.

The heat of the day was beginning to lie over the land around them now, the distant horizons shimmering as the dust devils cavorted over the plain.

Neil spurred his mount, rode out ahead of the train, knew that Jackson was close behind him. They reined their mounts on top of the curving crest of the hill that looked down on to the wide valley spread out before them, a vast stretch of land that lay all the way in front of them towards the mountains in the far distance where the red rays of the sun were just touching the ragged peaks with splashes of crimson.

'They'll have their beef cattle somewhere about,' he remarked tonelessly. 'Ought to be some of their men here, too, keeping an eye open.'

'You mean the Shermans?'

'That's right. Matt Hollard's spread is a hundred miles or so to the west of this one.'

'I'm not interested in Hollard, or Sherman,' said Jackson. He pointed back towards the straggling wagons. 'All I'm concerned with is getting that wagon train to California. You getting scared now that we're close to trouble?'

Neil lifted the reins and set his right foot hard in its stirrup, watched the hardness in the other's face, the wariness at the back of his eyes. With an effort he controlled the anger that had risen deep within him, choked it down, relaxed his hands where the right one had hovered for a fraction of a second just above the gun in the holster.

'I'm not afraid for myself, and you know it, Jackson,' he said tightly, forcing evenness into his tone. 'But there are women and children back there in those wagons, and we surely have to take them into consideration.'

'I'll answer for every one of them,' declared the big man dispassionately.

He turned his head, looked out over the plain, then stiffened abruptly in his saddle, nodded towards the open valley below them.

'Looks as though there may be trouble sooner than we think.'

A small curtain of dust moved towards them, down on the plain, and Neil saw the three riders spurring their horses in their direction. He nodded in agreement.

'Sherman's men,' he said tonelessly. 'They may decide to give us a warning to turn back while we have the chance; but it's more likely that they'll try to gun us down, then ride back with the warning to Sherman. Once they get there, a score or more will ride out on Sherman's orders to destroy the train.'

The three riders set their mounts at the slope of the hill, rode up to the crest. The horses they sat were lean and hard, the saddles worn. Each man wore his guns low and their eyes checked the two men sitting there, then flickered in the direction of the slowly advancing wagon train down below on the other side of the hill.

'You know that this spread belongs to Jesse Sherman,' murmured one of the men silkily. 'He doesn't like homesteaders moving across it.'

For a long moment Jackson stared at the three men facing him.

'We're driving straight across,' he said flatly. 'Do you figure on trying to stop us?'

For an instant there was a perplexed consternation on the face of the first man, then his eyes narrowed to mere slits and he sat a little straighter in the saddle. His eyes were as empty and emotionless as those of a snake, and the thin cruel mouth was compressed to a mere slit.

'Reckon you two *hombres* have made a big

mistake,' he grated harshly.

Not once did his gaze leave Neil's face, and it was as if he had instantly recognised that it was he, and not the bigger man, who was the more dangerous of the two.

Neil said: 'Suppose you prove that, mister,' speaking in an even steady voice.

This one, and possibly the other two, would be fast men with a gun, he reflected. All three were undoubtedly professional killers, deliberately hired by Sherman to do any dirty work like this for him. Men he could trust because only here, in his employ, would they be safe from the law. There would be wanted posters of these men in sheriffs' offices all over the territory, rewards out for them, dead or alive.

There was also an easiness about the way in which the three men sat their mounts and waited, quite obviously certain that they were facing a couple of men far slower with their guns than they were themselves.

The man's eyes were fixed on Neil's face, unblinking, steady. The other was one who watched a man's eyes for a sign that the other was beginning his draw. That way, thought Neil, he got the signal a split second before his opponent's hand began its downward move. It gave him an edge, one which had probably been sufficient to keep him alive so far through a dozen gunfights that he might otherwise have lost. A cocky gunfighter, with a strange warped sense of pride, who would not draw first unless he was sure that the man he faced was probably faster than he was.

Neil could almost read the uneasy balance of the other's thoughts, the rapid weighing of his chances. Then, suddenly, the man's stretched patience was gone. His hand moved, striking down for the gun at his belt with the speed of a rattler and, as he moved, so did the two men with him, their hands moving almost in unison.

Even as their guns lifted into line, two guns threw death at the gunmen, both guns blazing as one. The first man went down grabbing at his chest, the gun tilting from his hand, hitting the dirt a second before he did. The other two sat for a moment, bolt upright in their saddles, expressions of stunned amazement on their hard features. Then they slumped forward in their saddles, arms hanging loosely over the pommels for an instant before they, too, fell and lay still, their mounts shying away. Then there was silence; a dark silence that crowded in on the two men at the top of the low hill.

Slowly, eyes wider than before, Jackson turned to face Neil, then dropped his gaze to where the smoke still rose from the twin guns in the other's hands.

Roughly almost, Neil pouched them, sat forward a little, elbows on the saddle, staring down at the still things on the ground only a little distance away. Guns had spoken on that quiet hill overlooking the vastness of the plain, guns held in the hands of a master craftsman, hands which had moved faster than the eye could follow and had shot to kill.

'If you're thinking that this might stop the others from attacking us, then you're wrong,' said Neil softly, and his words fell into the deep and muffling silence all about them. 'Sherman will see us all dead for this – and even if we do get through, we'll have to face Matt Hollard and his gunhawks.'

Jackson gave a quick little nod, then tightened his mouth.

'We'll face 'em,' he said, with a growing confidence in his voice. 'And I take back all I said about you being scared to go on.'

'I still think you're a fool.' Neil's voice was still quiet. 'This is some of the worst country in the whole of the United States, and by the time we've crossed to the border the weather will have changed, it'll be winter, and only a fool would attempt to cross those mountains once the winter snows start.'

'We'll face up to that when it comes,' muttered Jackson.

He pulled hard on the reins, wheeled his mount and rode back down the slope towards the wagon train.

Moving past the hill, the wagons drove westward. The sun climbed up into the zenith, a flaming disc of fire, burning their skin, the heat shocking back at them from the plain in dizzying waves.

They nooned in the lee of a tall canyon but there was no shade there, and men sweated and cursed, drooped in their saddles, rubbing the white dust out of their eyes.

There was mesquite and low cactus here and, further on, from the edge of the camp, Neil could make out where the scrub oak began, dense growths which could give concealment to a whole army of gunhawks.

This was a place of weirdly etched buttes and narrow gorges, fluted and carved by wind and sand, a rugged and inhospitable stretch of country legally belonging to no man, but claimed by Jesse Sherman, anxious to protect his stretch of grassland some distance to the west.

The drive began again during the afternoon. There was no place there to make camp that day and both Jackson and Neil were anxious to move on. Deep in the choking dust through which the horses made their way and the wooden wheels of the wagons rolled, the train moved forward in single file.

Jackson had taken his place on the seat of the lead wagon again and at times he waved encouragement to the others following behind. There were women seated beside the menfolk, Neil noticed, sitting tall in the saddle as he rode a little distance away, women who carried the long-barrelled repeater rifles in their hands, women who would not be afraid to fight alongside their menfolk if the going got tough.

But he still felt a little uneasy in his mind. Whether or not they were prepared to fight, whether or not they had more rifles and six-guns among them than the band of gunhawks that Sherman would un-doubtedly throw against them, he doubted the ability of these people to fight against professional killers, and there was also the one inescapable fact that even if they did succeed in driving these men off, even if they managed to fight their way through, not only Sherman's country, but Hollard's spread further along the route, by that time their numbers would be so depleted, their stores at rock bottom, that the survivors would lack the courage or the stomach to fight off the raiding border gangs who were even more dangerous than the gunhawks they were likely to see here.

On top of that, there would be the long winter days up in the mountains, seeking a place to camp, shelter from the raging blizzards that swept those icy slopes, and then– But what was the use in going on, thinking along those lines? If everyone paused to consider the difficulties that faced them, no one would ever have ventured out into this wild, untamed country in the first place.

He shrugged off the thoughts, rested himself more easily in the saddle, let the sorrel pick its own gait. When a man had a long way to ride, the best way was the slow way.

As he rode, his eyes three-quarter lidded to shield off the all-pervading glare, he saw all there was to be seen right out to the shimmering horizons, and he speculated long on the shape of the buttes or the twisted course of a deep ravine with steep razor-backed sides, seeking out any places where a man with a rifle might lie concealed, his mind drawn inward in the manner of a man who often rode alone.

For the men rolling west with the wagons, it might appear that this was good country, and that the country that lay directly ahead was even better, with rich green grass, watered by great rivers, territory where there could be a coolness that one could not find out here in the middle of the scorched wilderness.

For him, however, the opposite was the truth. With the trees and grass there would be danger. There it would be impossible to see far, and death could be very close and a man would never suspect its presence until it was too late.

And there was another danger, one which came from the cattle that roamed these prairie lands. They were unused to the wagons, would be moving on their muscle, and the slightest wrong move, or the slightest prompting by Sherman's men herding them, could begin a stampede. His mind baulked at the thought, racing ahead, visualising what could happen if this slow-moving wagon train found itself in the path of a stampeding herd. There would be nothing whatever left of them by the time those countless tons of muscle and beef had smashed their way through the wagons.

He set a spur against the flank of his sorrel and rode forward, watchful, recognising the places where danger might lie in hiding, but the long heat of the afternoon passed without incident. They saw nothing that moved on the plain around them and, at their backs, the dust settled slowly, dust kicked up by the hooves of the horses and the churning wheels of the wagons.

There had been dust and heat and a blazing sun, but now, slowly, that sun was descending towards the undulating skyline of the west where the tall peaks of the mountains still seemed as distant, as far off, as ever. Neil estimated that they had moved perhaps ten miles that day, good going considering the fact that most of the wagons had a couple of cows tethered to the back, and at best the wagons themselves could move only slowly and ponderously on their creaking axles.

Night came out of the east. The sky overhead purpled, then grew dark, and the stars stood out in their thousands, a vast curve of powdered light right down to the far horizons. Twin fires blazed in the camp, but now that they were well inside Sherman territory, Neil placed more men on watch and himself rode the perimeter of the camp, knowing that there would be little sleep for him that night, not with the ever-present possibility of a surprise attack lying heavy on his mind.

Jackson and Sam Jessup moved forward to join him in the cold darkness. Caught in silhouette by the faint light of the half-moon, horses and riders blended as dark shadows across the uneven ground. Neil sat quite still and waited.

'You reckon there might be trouble during the night?' asked Jessup quietly.

'Could be.' Neil nodded. 'This isn't the best place to make camp with gunslingers like Sherman's men around. They'll have found those three men back there by now and soon they'll come looking for revenge.'

The big man was silent for a moment, pondering on the other's words. Then he shifted himself in his saddle.

'Just what kind of a man is this Jesse Sherman?' he asked, staring off into the darkness that lay all about them.

There was a quick glance from Neil.

'He's ruthless, determined. Came out here just after the finish of the war. They say he came from somewhere up north, but nobody knows much about him. Built up a cattle empire from almost nothing; and a man has to be ruthless to do a thing like that. He knows that sooner or later there'll be nesters moving in, that the Government will break up the big stretches of land, and he's determined to resist that with every means at his command. And if that means bringing in every gunslinger and killer this side of the Rio Grande, then he'll do it. He'll offer them safety so long as they stay on his land and obey the orders he gives. They do all of the killing for him and make sure that nobody tries to settle on the land, or even to cross it as we're doing now.

'In return, he keeps them from the law. They don't have to keep on runnin' and driftin' from state to state, always one jump ahead of a United States Marshal.'

Jackson mused on that for some time, then nodded his great head.

'And Neil Roberts – what kind of a man is he?'

Neil hesitated for the barest fraction of a second, almost as if caught off balance by the question. Then he shrugged his shoulders nonchalantly.

'Sometimes I discover myself wondering about him,' he said soberly. 'Wonder why he does what he does. Why he kills as he does – and where he's really going. Then again, I wonder if he'll ever get there, wherever it is.'

There was a loud bellow of a laugh from Jackson. He gave a quick nod.

'Like I said when we first met, Roberts – I like you. And after what happened on that hill back there, I'm glad that you're with us and not against us.'

Behind them where the fires were dying slowly, there was a faint snicker of a horse, a sudden movement, then silence once more.

Neil continued to sit tall and straight in the saddle, staring around him, eyes probing the darkness, looking for any faint shadow or a vaguely seen cloud of dust in the distance; ears straining to pick up the faint thunder of horses moving over the flat prairie, but there was nothing, and gradually he forced himself to relax.

He had figured that if Sherman's men had found the bodies of their three companions up there on the hill, perhaps ten, twelve miles to the east, they would follow the easily seen trail of the wagon train and attack after dark, when they would have the advantage of surprise. The fact that there was no sign of them worried him more than if they had swung in from the east and ridden down on the sleeping train, guns blazing. He rode on, circling the wagons in the darkness, the cold seeping through into his bones.

2

Danger at Noon

Morning, and the train moved out of camp, rolled on to the west. It was hard driving for the men and women on the wagons, hard, monotonous and mean. The dust of the hard ground, lifted by the ploughing hooves of the horses, hung thick and white in the air, worked its way into the folds of the skin, itching and irritating, gummed up the lips and burned the eyes so that it was impossible to see properly at the end of the first hour.

Already the heat pressure was rising swiftly, but this time, Neil noticed there was something different about the sun. It no longer shone brilliantly in the east. Instead, there seemed to be a dullish, eye-searing haze surrounding it, a haze that spread up from the horizon, thickening as the minutes dragged themselves into hours. The air was utterly still and windless, an expectant calm that began to eat at his nerves as he rode the edge of the trail.

The sky in front of them now carried an answering glaze as if the blue polish of the sky had been scoured and braided, giving it a curiously threatening look. He turned his horse, rode in closer to the wagon and their straining teams.

At the rear of the train, where the dust hung thickest in the air, he rode alongside the wagon, eyes slitted against the sickening glare. There was a woman riding on the tongue, holding the reins tightly in her hands, and beside her a boy of perhaps eleven or twelve, freckle-faced, bright-eyed. Neil noticed the way they kept flicking their glance towards the heavens, knew that they, too, had noticed the storm that was brewing down there close to the horizon, that they were as worried about it as he himself.

Virginia Millais and her son Johnny had, according to Jackson, joined the train at Boston, were going west to join her husband in California. It was a long and hard journey for a woman and a boy, he reflected, as he rode alongside the wagon, watching the way in which the woman handled the team, noticing the rifle cradled in the boy's arms.

He leaned forward with one arm resting on the rope-burned pommel while the woman turned and eyed him with a faintly apprehensive smile on her lips. She gestured to the south-west.

'What do you think that means, Mister Roberts?' she asked quietly.

'Trouble, I'm afraid,' he answered slowly. 'There's a storm coming up, Ma'am, a bad one. I reckon it ought to hit us around noon at the rate it's travelling. We may be lucky and get only the fringe of it, but that's going to be bad.'

'It looks ominous.'

'Dust storm,' nodded Neil musingly. 'Often blows up in these parts at this time of the year. Better make certain that you keep the canvas tightly closed or you'll spend the rest of the journey trying to get rid of the sand in there. It will help, too, to keep your faces covered with kerchiefs, or you'll find it difficult to breathe when it does hit us.'

They nodded.

'Do you intend to stop the train when it comes?'

Neil shook his head. 'Won't do any good to stop, Ma'am. We'll just keep them moving. That way we'll get through it quicker. But whatever happens, make sure that you keep up with the others. If you drop behind and lose sight of the wagon in front of you, you'll be lost in minutes, and when the storm blows itself out we may never find you.'

He spurred his mount, rode swiftly along the line of wagons, giving the same warning, the same advice, to each of the drivers, making sure that they understood, sitting his sorrel while they tied down the canvas. He doubted if any of them had been through a real dust storm before, if any of them really knew what it was like, those millions of swirling yellow grains, hurled by a shrieking, howling wind that blew endlessly and with a terrible force, cutting into a man's body, making it almost impossible for him to move forward against it, even if he bent himself into the wind. It would be almost as bad for the animals. They, too, would be forced to keep moving into it. He threw a wary eye in the direction of the approaching storm, felt a wave of apprehension go through him.

An hour passed. Still the storm had not reached them, the air hung heavy and oppressive, with the stillness that came before the storm.

Neil reached the head of the train where Jackson sat huge and square on the tongue of the wagon, a bull of a man, the hands that held the reins heavy across the backs, with black hairs along the wrist that glistened in the diffuse sunlight.

46

'I've told them all to close it up,' Neil said tightly. 'We're going to get that storm in less than an hour now, and it won't be easy to see when it does hit us. I don't want to lose any wagons.'

It was almost as if the other hadn't heard the words. His eyes looked due west, reaching out over the flatlands to where the mountains lifted sheer towards the sky on the horizon. But now they did not stand out clearly as they had on previous days, their outline etched darkly against the blue heavens. Now it was difficult to see them at all. Occasionally it was just possible to glimpse a tall peak that thrust itself up out of the flatness of the plains. Then it would be lost again as the dust storm blotted it out completely, erasing it as if some painter had come along and made some swift strikes with his brush, wiping it off the broad canvas.

In spite of the fact that he knew what to expect, that he had ridden storms such as this before, Neil felt himself tensing in the saddle as the curtain of yellow-white haze swept closer. Now it was so near that it was possible to see it moving, to see the strangely intermingled draperies that formed within its diffuse boundaries; rather like the sheets of dark rain that could be seen whenever the summer thunderstorms rolled in over the mountains, but more subtle and ominous.

The wind began to rise, plucking a little at the sleeves of his jacket, lifting the sand and dust from the ground all about them, hurling it over the plain in a faint sheet of yellow.

At their backs the sun had climbed higher into the darkening sky, but although it was now virtually at its zenith and the heat pressure lay on everything like the press of some hot, invisible hand, it was difficult to see the sun clearly. It was hidden now behind the thickening cloud of sand that came sweeping in from the far horizons. It was a long silence that clung about the wagon train now as it rumbled slowly forward at a snail-like pace, the wheels creaking and groaning, the axles grinding, the occasional slap of the reins against the rumps of the horses. The silence was made even more ominous and pronounced by the faint but rising shriek of the strengthening wind. Neil rode back along the train strung out over nearly half a mile of prairie, urging them to close up, shouting his warnings now at the top of his voice to make himself heard above the sickening howl of the wind in his ears.

The storm was on them with a suddenness that took everyone by surprise. One moment it seemed to be hanging back, lying low on the western horizon; the next it had closed in on them from all sides, blinding, searing the flesh wherever it was exposed, clogging the mouth and nostrils, making eyes useless, the countless millions of irritating grains working their way into the folds of the skin, into the necks and sleeves of tunics and dresses, finding its way into a million crevices along the wagons. The horses stumbled forward, weary animals, moving into that terrible yellow wall of sand and dust.

Head lowered, his bandana over the lower half of his face, eyes narrowed to mere slits, trying desperately to draw pure air into his aching lungs, Neil rode up and down the entire length of the train, keeping it in motion, knowing inwardly with a sick certainty that the moment one of those wagons stopped, or got itself bogged down in the drifting sand, they were finished. He would have to call a halt then, and at the moment that was the last thing he wanted to do. So long as he could keep them moving forward, it lessened the time they would be in the middle of that terrible storm.

How long it would take to blow itself out

he did not know. Sometimes they lasted for less than an hour, at others they could blow for the best part of a day. The ground was as level as a table, and there were no hills where they could shelter while the storm blew itself out around them.

The racing yellow cloud snapped across the last sliver of blue-grey sky and the sun was blotted out entirely now so that they moved in a strange and frightening half-world of dimness and discomfort. There was a terrible savagery in that storm as if nature were daring men to defy her, to put their strength against hers. Primitive and raw, the dust storm swept along the whole length of the train, a solid blanket of grains hurled by the wind. It was old to him, having experienced it before, but still frightening. The wind was a roaring thunder in his ears, blotting out all other sound. He fought to keep his head lifted, pushed his sight as far as possible into the yellowness that surrounded him. Less than ten feet away he could just make out the canvas top of the nearest wagon, swaying from side to side as the driver, crouched down low on the tongue, urged the horses forward as fast as they could go. But already they had slowed to a crawl and nothing on earth, Neil knew, would encourage them to go any faster now. He tried to see the wagon directly ahead, could see nothing at first, then barely made out the vaguely seen shape that appeared and then vanished tantalisingly between great gusts of dust.

It was going to be very difficult, if not utterly impossible for them to keep together. He knew that with a sudden certainty and felt a sharp sense of loss at the back of his mind, tightening the muscles of his ribs.

Turning his mount, he rode back along the trail. The wind was now at his back, he was riding with the storm, able to breathe just a little more easily. He passed four wagons, glimpsed the men and women huddled down on the seats, holding on for grim death as they humped and swayed from side to side, the fear-crazed horses hauling savagely on the reins so that it was all the men could do to keep them in check.

Neil felt the sickness in the pit of his stomach growing as he made his way to the very end of the train. He passed the last but one wagon, then pushed his way forward, eyes peering under the lowered black brows, searching for any sign of the last wagon in the train, for Virginia Millais and her son. He picked his way forward slowly and carefully. It was out of the question to try to pick up the sound of the wagon above the high-pitched shriek of the wind in his ears. He had to rely on seeing it through that whirling, sweeping wall of yellow.

The minutes lengthened and still there was no sign of the wagon. Was it possible that he himself had worked his way off the trail, that he was moving around in a circle, unable to orientate himself? Had he passed within a few yards of it and yet not seen it, not even known of its presence there?

He turned his head in every direction, trying to make out anything that moved, a sense of terrible urgency riding him now. He knew that he had to find that wagon within the next five minutes or the chances were that he might never find it again. There was no sign that the storm was abating, blowing itself out; the wind still blew with a fierceness that snatched away his breath, and there was no let-up in the fury of the storm.

Four minutes later, when he was on the point of giving up, of turning his sorrel back into the teeth of the storm, trying to search in another direction, he caught a fragmentary glimpse of something dark, something only vaguely seen on his right. Swinging the head of the sorrel towards it, he kicked in his spurs, felt the horse bound under him, feet sliding a little in the loose sand underfoot.

A moment later the unmistakable shape of the wagon materialised out of the yellow gloom, directly in front of him. He could just see the figure of the woman, her face swathed in a broad handkerchief, still gripping the reins. The wheels were barely moving, the two horses straining clumsily and awkwardly.

Scarcely pausing to think, Neil turned his stud, brought the sorrel alongside the wagon, then slid out of the saddle, coming up beside the woman in a single, smooth movement. He took the reins from her as she moved, unresisting, further along the seat. There was no sign of the boy and Neil guessed that he had taken shelter from the storm inside the wagon.

A moment while Neil's hand flicked the long whip against the hides of the horses, a moment while they seemed to hesitate. Then they strained forward and the wagon began to roll more quickly, edging its way in the direction Neil judged the rest of the wagon train to be.

It was quite impossible to see the trail, impossible to guess if they were headed in the right direction. All he could do at that moment was to keep the horses moving into the storm, trust that the wind had not changed direction, and that the rest of the train was still doing the same. There were so many things which could go wrong, he knew, and the chances were great that once the storm lifted they would find themselves isolated, with no sign of the wagon train.

'Where in God's name are the others?' called the woman. 'We lost sight of them just after the storm began.'

'They'll be just up ahead,' he shouted reassuringly, trying to look confident in spite of the growing sense of uneasiness in him. 'All we can do now is ride out the storm, wait for it to die down. Then we'll join the others. They won't be able to make very good time, either.'

'I told Johnny to stay back there, out of the way.'

She leaned forward a little, only the slits of her eyes showing over the kerchief.

Slowly they moved into the heart of the gigantic storm that swept over the wide, stretching distances of the plain, the sky darkened, the triumphant sound of the wind a harsh, endless shriek in the ears, the rustling of millions of individual grains of sand grinding along the wagon, tearing at the canvas, threatening to rip it into shreds. Even the ground underfoot seemed to be sliding and shaking as if the sea were rippling about them, long waves moving in and then vanishing behind the wagon. It was an incredible thing, a frightening thing, nature gone wild and turned insane.

The long minutes passed, still the storm blew about them in its full and awesome fury. Neil found it becoming more difficult to breathe, and every breath that he did take burned like fire in his aching lungs, pounded in his throat and chest.

No sight of the other wagons in the train, no distant sound in their ears for all lesser sounds were blotted out by the terrible shriek of the wind, the grating of the sand on the metal and canvas of the wagon. It was impossible even to talk, for the words were torn from their lips and tossed into the yellow haze.

Out of the corner of his vision, Neil saw the woman's face, lowered against the whirling dust, tight with fear and apprehension. He could guess at the thoughts that must have been passing through her mind at that moment. They were lost. They did not even know if they were still on the trail. There were no landmarks they could see, and it was as if they were utterly isolated in that tremendous, howling wilderness of yellow dust and alkali.

'What can we do now?' The woman turned and shouted the words in his ear, bending close so that he might hear her.

He shook his head. 'Nothing for the moment. We'll just have to ride out the storm and hope we can pick up the others once it blows itself out. Maybe it would be easier for you inside. I'll call you if I need you.'

She shot him a thankful glance, turned and moved into the wagon, pulling the thick canvas tightly over the opening. Neil turned on the tongue of the wagon, holding the leather tightly in his hands. The horses moved forward slowly now, fighting their way through the dancing, swirling haze that roared about them, choking and blinding. His own sorrel moved alongside the wagon. It needed no rope to tether it to the back.

There were long moments now, minutes which dragged themselves out into individual eternities of uncomfortable straining, choking agony. Leaning forward against the thrusting pressure of the storm, Neil pushed his sight through the yellow haze, looking for any sign of the other wagons.

Deep down inside, he knew that it would be unlikely that he would catch any glimpse of them until the storm died, blew itself out. Even then there was the possibility that he was driving the wagon in a tight circle, was now miles from the others. There was the chance that they, too, had become scattered, even though he had impressed on them the necessity for keeping close to each other, within sight of the wagon in front.

In the past too many wagons had been lost entirely in dust storms such as this whenever they blazed their way over the stretching wilderness, and they had not been found until months, perhaps years, later, with the bleached bones telling their own pathetic story of men and women who had died many miles from the nearest waterhole, who had wandered through the sun-caked desert until they had died of thirst.

If there was a hell anywhere, he thought savagely, surely this was it. This terrible curtain of choking dust which never once let up in its mad whine, which shut off all sight, worked its way painfully into the folds of the skin, mingled irritatingly with the sweat that coursed down the cheeks and along the muscles of his back and chest, worked into his clothing so that there was not a single inch of his flesh which was not on fire with the itching particles that tore and chafed at his body.

Back inside the wagon it would be little better. It had been a futile gesture telling the woman to go inside. The sand would find its way everywhere, and within minutes of the storm blowing up and swallowing them in its yellow mist, the interior of the wagons would be covered with sand and alkali, not a single inch escaping.

The wagon lurched as one of the wheels hit an upthrusting boulder. For a second it threatened to tilt over on to its side, and Neil fought savagely to right it. His eyes were blinking as he tried to see in front of him. They were driving over rough, uneven terrain now, not the kind of smooth, flat ground he expected on the trail. Another lurch as he fought for control. Then the canvas at his back parted, was twitched aside, and Virginia Millais peered out at him. Her eyes were wide now, staring up at him in a brief moment of brilliance.

Suddenly frightened eyes. Then her gaze flickered towards the rearing canyon walls that suddenly loomed up in front of them, crushing in on either side of the wagon. Neil sucked in a sharp breath, cursed himself for not realising this possible reason for the sudden increase in the shrieking howl of the wind. That sudden sharp jump in its speed ought to have warned him that the wind was moving along a constricted path, that they were entering a narrow gorge.

Clumsily, awkwardly, the wagon moved between the red sandstone walls. He tried to see where they were going, knowing now that the only thing he could do was to let the horses pick their own gait, choose their own path, rely on that strange animal instinct which might guide them through this new danger.

'Get back in there,' Neil yelled at the top of his voice. He pulled hard on the leather as one of the horses reared, threatened to bolt. He did not even bother to turn his head to see if she had obeyed him. Everything now depended on them being able to ease their way between these tall walls of sandstone, trusting that it was not a box canyon, that at the end of it they would find a dead end.

The wagon lurched as the rough surface of the canyon wall slid by less than an inch on one side. His sorrel had dropped behind. Perhaps it had already taken fright and bolted into the storm. The thought crossed his mind briefly, then he thrust it away. If that had happened, there was certainly nothing he could do about it now.

Somehow they had to work their way out of this canyon, out into more open country. There, with the immediate danger lessened, it might be possible for them to ride out the storm. That they were well off the trail, he now realised. But there was nothing for them now but to go on and trust to Providence that they were not too far away, that they would find themselves in sight of the others when the storm passed.

Thunder from the roaring sweep of the wind. Thunder from the millions of red and yellow grains. His ears hurt with the sound of it. His eyes burned as if they were on fire, the dust having worked its way under the lids, blinding and sore every time he blinked.

If only it were possible to see, he would have felt easier in his mind. It was the fact that his vision was limited to less than five yards that added immeasurably to the danger.

Then, as suddenly as it had begun, the storm was leaving. Neil lifted his head slowly. The whine of the wind was no longer quite as loud or as shrill as it had been just a few minutes earlier. For a few seconds he had the impression that it was nothing more than his imagination. Then he found that he could make out the far end of the canyon, that directly in front of them the floor of the ravine widened, the rearing walls moving away from the trail, and fifty yards ahead lay open country. The sky was noticeably lighter now. The ominous yellowness was fading appreciably, and he could make out the position of the sun overhead, a dull patch of light that was growing brighter with every passing second.

He pushed the kerchief tighter around his face, breathing through it. As a filter against the whirling grains, it was remarkably efficient, but it tended to become clogged with the alkali, rubbing his cheeks and chin raw and making it difficult to breathe through it after some minutes.

Narrowing his eyes, he stared straight in front of him. As he watched, the dark yellow curtain rolled across the sky, the ochre colour changed swiftly to blue, and the sun came out, harsh and brilliant, glaring down at them from the broad heavens. Jerking the kerchief from around his face, he sucked in deep breaths of clean, pure air, expanding his chest as he drew it down into his lungs. Gradually the tight ache in his body went away, he found himself able to see more clearly, although there was still a dull red haze hovering in front of his vision.

They came out into the open country and he reined the horses, standing on the wooden tongue of the wagon, shading his eyes against the harsh glare of the sun, peering in all directions, looking for the other wagons in the train. Virginia Millais stepped out through the opening in the canvas. Her face was streaked with sand and dust, and it had worked its way into her long hair. She licked her dry, cracked lips and rubbed at her cheeks absently.

'Can you see any sign of the others, Mister Roberts?' she asked in a throaty voice, blinking her eyes against the glare.

Slowly he shook his head.

'We must have wandered some way off the trail, Ma'am,' he said. 'Wouldn't have thought they would be too far away. The storm would've slowed them just as much as it did us, and this is pretty open country hereabouts. Ought to be able to spot 'em if they're anywhere within fifteen miles or so.'

'I don't see them.'

'They've got to be around somewhere.' He clambered down from the wagon. 'We'll have to find 'em before dark. By morning they could be clear into the next state, and then we'll never catch up with 'em.'

'What do you intend to do? You're not leaving us here, are you?'

There was a note of apprehensive fear in her voice now as she looked at him anxiously. Neil had moved away from the wagon, then he turned.

'Have no fear of that, Ma'am, but I reckon there ain't no chance of picking that train out from down here. I was thinking that maybe if I was to climb up to the top of that ravine I might get a better view over the country around here, might be able to pick 'em out more easily. There's just the chance that we made even better time than they did, and they're still moving up behind us. If that's so, we won't see 'em until they get level with us, and it might be dark by then.'

He turned and began to make his way up the steep, rough slope where the sheer walls of the canyon lifted out of the flatness of the desert. Behind them, in the direction they had just travelled, it was impossible to see anything, for the ravine blocked off all vision. It was hard work, climbing that steep slope. His fingers clawed and hooked on to outjutting spurs of rock as he hauled himself up, feet searching for tiny footholds where he could find them. More than once his feet slipped from under him and he was forced to hang there by his hands, shoulder muscles aching with the tearing strain of taking his whole weight on his arms.

Whipping himself around, grasping tightly at the ledge of rock above his head, he swung outward into space and downward, feet sliding off the inch-wide ledge on which he had been standing. For a split second his fingers threatened to loose their hold, sending him pitching downward to the floor of the canyon some forty feet below him. He dropped until his chest scraped hard on the jagged rock, the impact knocking all of the wind out of his body. Desperately he fought to retain his hold, heaving himself upward with all of the strength in his arm and shoulder muscles, drawing agonising gulps of air down into his straining lungs.

His vision blurred for a moment. Then he managed to get one elbow hooked over the sharp edge of the ledge above him and hung there for what seemed an eternity – but which could only have been a few seconds – his feet digging against the hard surface of the sandstone, toes kicking savagely as he struggled to make a hole for himself, a slight foothold in the otherwise completely smooth surface.

Swiftly he pulled himself up a couple of inches, until he had his other elbow over the ledge, and for the moment he had anchored himself securely to the face of the canyon wall.

Gradually, moving his toes up and down, he found lodgement for his feet, lifted himself slowly and gently, an inch at a time, his arms and elbows taking the strain from the very insecure foothold he had found for himself. A pause, then he gathered his strength, gritted his teeth tightly in his head and made the upward lunge that carried him on to the ledge, where he crawled to safety.

Sitting upright, he brushed the filming of sweat from his forehead with the back of his sleeve, then glanced above him. The top of the canyon was now less than twelve feet away, but here the rocky wall bulged outward a little, like a huge wave of stone, frozen just at the very moment of breaking. It was not going to be an easy matter easing his way around that shoulder of rock, he reflected, but if he wanted to reach the top it had to be done, and there was no sense in sitting there and thinking about it, wasting precious minutes.

He glanced down for a moment and could just make out the shape of the wagon standing where he had left it, with the figure of Virginia Millais staring up at him, her head tilted back in the sunlight so that she could see him better. He saw that the canvas flap of the wagon had been thrown back and Johnny Millais was peering up at him too, eyes shaded, squinting up against the harsh glare of the burning sunlight.

He drew in a deep breath, flexed his hands for a moment, then rose carefully to his feet, stood quite still for a moment on the narrow ledge, finding a firm and secure foothold before he made his final attempt on the rocky face.

Gingerly he edged his heels back until they were poised over the very edge of the ledge, shuffling them a little until he was sure of his stance; then he moved around the blistered, bulging face of rock, body flattened against the sandstone, his belly drawn in until it seemed to be touching his backbone.

Inching sideways, he found the narrow gully he had hoped might be there, knew that it would be relatively simple to work his way up it now. Pulling himself up with caution, he finally reached the top and threw himself forward, rolling a little way to make certain that he was well away from the lip of the canyon, before sitting up and staring about him.

Far off to the south-east he could just make out the misty cloud of the storm as it receded over the face of the desert. It stretched across a vast stretch of country and, from that distance, it seemed to be in no real hurry to move.

Then he lowered his gaze and almost gasped out aloud in his relief. Down there, perhaps two, three miles away and, as he had half-suspected, behind them, were the other wagons, a string of dark dots, partially hidden in the dust of their own drag, edging forward, one behind the other. He reckoned that in less than half an hour they would have drawn level with the canyon, but about a mile to the south.

Relief from the pressing feeling that they were completely lost was so great that for several moments he could do nothing but stare out at them, holding his breath. He guessed that, having to maintain contact with each other and knowing that the danger of getting lost was ever-present, Clem Jackson had deliberately slowed their pace. He let his breath go in a long sigh, waved an arm to the woman down below, saw her lift her right arm in answer. Then he began his descent. Going down was, if anything, even more difficult and hazardous than the climb had been but somehow he made it without mishap and walked over to Virginia Millais.

'They're over in that direction.' He pointed. 'About two miles away. I reckon we ought to meet up with them in an hour or so. They'll probably spot us the minute we get clear of these rocks. They've been hiding us until now.'

She nodded slowly and the utter relief showed clearly on her face. Her hand brushed some of the dust from her cheeks and lips, and she blinked it away from around her eyes.

They went back to the wagon, Neil hitched his sorrel to the back, and they moved off, heading into the sun glare. The heat lay like a vast pressure over the mesquite-dotted desert now and he reached down for the canteen nearby, offered it to Virginia first, then took a deep drink himself feeling the warm, brackish liquid trickle down his throat in a slow, refreshing stream. His dry, parched mouth absorbed a lot of it even before it reached his throat, but after a moment he felt better and his swollen tongue moved more easily around his mouth and lips.

They rode out from the deep shadow of the canyon, headed for the other wagons which could be clearly seen now. It was too far away for either of them to be sure whether they had been seen by any of the others, but as they drew nearer Neil saw that the line of wagons was turning slowly, heading in their direction.

Then they were near enough to make out the large figure of Clem Jackson, seated on the front of the leading wagon, his huge hand lifted in greeting. They came up to the others, Neil pulling sharply on the leather.

'We thought you were lost,' boomed Jackson's loud voice. 'What happened back there?'

'Lost contact with you during the storm. Only thing to do was to keep on going and hope to find you again when it blew over. We finished up in that narrow canyon yonder, but I managed to spot you from the top. We must have drifted some ways from the trail.'

The other nodded his huge head in agreement. He turned his head and stared towards the west, where the mountains in the distance were as far off as ever, still snuggling down on the skyline, dull blue in the streaming sunlight.

'Where do you reckon we ought to make

camp, Roberts? This don't look too good a place to me, not with that ravine less than two miles away. Anybody could be hiding there, and we'd know nothing about it.'

It was true; they would have to continue driving the tired animals further, through all of the heat of the long afternoon and the early evening. He wondered how far the horses would go before they fell in the traces. The storm would have taken far more out of them than was visible on the surface. The biting, scouring sand grains would have worked their way into the animals' throats and lungs, tearing, clogging and abrading. If they didn't rest up soon, get plenty of water, it might mean the end of some of them.

'Keep them moving,' he said quietly. 'We'll camp as soon as we get to an open space, or near water.'

3

Trail West

Night reached across the heavens from the east and the train camped on the banks of a small, shallow stream that came bubbling down between high banks of hard mud from the north. On the far side the ground rose steeply and became more rugged, and here and there were patches of dense forest, first-year pine as far as Neil could make out — and this presented more danger to them. True, it would offer them shade from the burning, blistering heat of the sun and the ground underfoot would be easier, but there was too much shelter for any of Sherman's men, too close to the trail, so that they might attack without warning. It meant that they would have to ride with eyes and ears open continually, that he would have to scout ahead of the train as it rumbled slowly west through this country. They were getting closer to the Sherman ranch now, and they could expect trouble, big trouble, at any time, once they crossed the stream. But for the time being, for that night, this was undoubtedly the best place they had found so far for making camp.

The men drew lots for the first night guard and the quiet voices of the unlucky pair could be heard in the darkness on the edge of the camp. The fire burned low and then went out unheeded. There was no point in keeping the fire going that night. Although the Conestoga wagons themselves would be readily spotted, even in the darkness, a fire would give away their position to watching eyes quite easily, and there seemed little reason for pinpointing their presence as accurately as that.

There was action down at the water's edge as men scrubbed the dust and alkali from their bodies, the cold water burning and stinging their skin where it had been scorched by the sun through the thick, coating of dust. Jackson cursed softly as he rubbed at his arms and face, then straightened, shook his head like a dog coming out of the water, slicked his hair back with the tips of his fingers.

'This storm was somethin' I never want to go through again,' he growled throatily. He looked across at Neil. 'You bin through one of 'em before?'

Neil nodded. 'Several times,' he affirmed. 'Always they seem to get worse. Could be that it's because you forget what it was like the last time and you always seem to think that it wasn't too bad.'

'Don't reckon it will be like that from now on. We seem to have left the desert behind us.'

'There's still danger ahead.'

'Sherman's men?' The reply was a question.

'That's right. They may decide not to attack us until they're sure they can finish us. They won't be partial to risking their own necks when they can ambush us somewhere along that trail and cut us down without too much risk to themselves, and those trees up there will make an excellent place for an ambush.'

'That's more'n likely,' agreed Jackson.

He rubbed himself dry. They walked slowly back to the camp where the fires were little more than glowing embers in the darkness.

'I'll ride out at first light. Take a look-see, just in case.' He stood in front of the dying fire. 'If my hunch is right, they'll follow us for a little way into those trees. An Indian would lose his way out there in the desert if he tried to track us down and, after that storm, our tracks would be completely wiped out. That desert was made for fellas on the dodge.'

Jackson grinned broadly. 'You're right.'

He sank down on to his haunches by the glowing embers. The words were flat and cold. Neil sat down opposite the other and watched the huge man's eyes grow a mist as they stared out into the cold darkness, out over the stream, over the hills beyond as if he could see clear out over that vast and wild, untamed country, clear to the borders of California.

What was the other thinking, Neil wondered. Why was he so anxious to get to California? Men had found gold there, he knew, rich red gold, and there had been the usual rush from the east, wagon trains setting out across the face of a continent, thrusting the frontier westward, rolling it back across the page of American history. There had been this sudden movement from the East to the West, many thousands of people all heading in the same direction.

True, there were inevitably some who turned aside, found a place to their liking, and stayed. There were countless others who never made it at all. But some got through, though it could not be said that the trail westward had yet been blazed. Perhaps that was what Jackson was hoping for. To be the leader of the first large wagon train to blaze the trail westward.

'You still figure that you're doing the right thing, bringing this train out along this trail?' he asked softly, keeping his gaze fixed on the other's face.

Jackson looked up and there was something about his features which surprised Neil. It was as if a tiny devil had jumped up behind the other's eyes, stood there exposed and naked for a long moment before sinking back down into the depths again, out of sight. Then the big man's lips thinned, drew closer to the square teeth. 'It's the only thing we can do now,' he said harshly.

'I suppose that you realise you're risking the lives of everyone in these wagons?'

'I only know that I warned them all of the difficulties they might have to face and that if they paid to join the train, then I'd lead them all the way to California, but they had to stick the trail. There was to be no turning back no matter how hard it got, or how tough the going was. They knew that and they all agreed before we set out.'

'But I wonder whether any of them really

knew what lay in store for them. I know, because I've lived out here most of my life. I know the kind of men you'll find here, hard, ruthless men, most of them with no respect for the law, men who would kill and think nothing of it if it meant they got their own way. And there's nothing surer than that these men don't want any nesters here.'

Jackson set his lips into a tight, thin line.

'The country is growing up, Roberts. Sooner or later, everybody has got to be made to realise that. If we're to be a nation at all, the country has got to be settled, and by men and women like those in the wagons, not by the killers and outlaws who're here at the moment. The Government realises this, which is why they're making the land available to settlers.'

'Mebbe so. But the settlers are going to have to fight for every inch of that land, and most of them don't stand a chance against professional gunmen. You know that as well as I do.'

'Sure I know it. But there ain't a thing I can do about it. I'm being paid to lead them out to California. That's what I aim to do and I don't mean to let Sherman, or any of his hired killers, stop me.'

Neil lifted his brows a little, then shrugged.

He got heavily to his feet.

'I hope that none of us regret it,' he said. He shrugged. 'I reckon I'm going to catch up some sleep.'

He got his blanket and rolled himself into it, lying close to the fire, with his Colts within easy reach of his hands. Jackson remained sitting by the dying fire, staring morosely into the red embers. Despite the other's bold front, Neil guessed that he was inwardly uneasy, that he had been turning over in his mind many of the things he had mentioned. They had been plain lucky so far, luckier than they had deserved. Either those three dead men back there had not yet been missed or found, or Sherman's boys were playing it safe, taking their time, knowing that they would have plenty of opportunities to strike before the wagon trail left the Sherman spread.

In the morning, before most of the others were awake, he saddled his sorrel, then swung up, put his mount to the stream and forded it swiftly, pulling up the horse on the far bank. Here there was a slope of sparse, dry grass where the desert seemed reluctant to release its hold on the territory, stretching its dry, bony fingers across the water.

Presently he rode among the tall, straight

trees, felt the cool, sharp smell of the pines in his nostrils. It was cool here for the sun had not yet risen and the dawn was merely a brightening line of silver grey in the east. The place held a strange fascination, almost as if there were a secret there, but as he rode, keeping his eyes and ears open, he found nothing there, certainly nothing to indicate that anyone had ridden that trail recently.

Coming out into the open again, there was a gentle slope leading down into a wide, open plain and, in the distance, he could make out the cattle, a large herd, possibly two thousand head, grazing on the rich grass.

He sat saddle for a while, studying his situation, looking keenly about him. There was no sign of any herders with the cattle, they seemed to have been left to their own devices, which struck him instantly as odd. A herd that size would have men guarding it, unless Sherman was extremely sure of himself, knew that there would be no trouble.

But there was another thing which made him feel a trifle uneasy. The trail led down into that wide valley and the wagons would be forced to make their way past the herd. Those cattle might be on the mean side and would not be used to wagons.

Shrugging the thought away, he turned

back into the brush. Maybe at that very moment Sherman was planning to save him the trouble of trying to get the wagon train past those cattle.

It was grey dawn when he rode back into the trees, and he heard the sound in the near distance very clearly. Swiftly reining the sorrel, he leaned forward in the saddle, straining his ears, waiting for the sound to be repeated, but there was no further noise and he could see nothing. But he had been certain that he had heard a man's voice yelling orders.

Then, looking upwards, he discovered a man seated on the lip of the trail, high among the trees, less than three hundred feet away. Even as he stared at the other, the man brought a rifle to his shoulder, took quick aim and fired, the bullet striking the dirt of the trail wide of Neil's position. The sorrel flung up its head at the sharp, flat report of the rifle, then Neil had dug in his heels, making a run for it towards the nearest clump of trees, head low, lying over the saddle to present a more difficult target to the bushwhacker.

Another shot drummed through the air very close to his head and buried itself in the trunk of a nearby tree, slashing the brown bark away and revealing a deep gash in the trunk. Then Neil had flung himself from the saddle before the other could take aim again, his Colts whispering from their worn leather holsters, snapping into his hands, in spite of the jarring agony of the impact of hitting the ground, knocking the air from his lungs in a loud gasp.

He rolled over on to his side, brought up the guns and snapped a couple of shots in the direction of the man. The marksman on the rim of the trail continued to pump shots methodically into the brush close to where Neil lay, trying to seek out his target, laying a pattern of bullets into the rough foliage. It was clear that he had lost Neil for the moment, but the lead was flying disturbingly close and Neil knew that it was only a matter of time before the other hit him, or the sound of rifle shots brought more of these gunhawks running to the scene. It would not take them long to surround him, cut him off from the rest of the men with the train back across the stream.

The firing ceased for a moment. The marksman would be taking time to reload, he figured. Maybe he was working his way closer, too, trying to improve his position, get within sighting and killing range.

In the mesquite, the daylight brightened. Soon the sun would bound up from below the horizon, flooding everything in its harsh light, and he would find it more difficult to get away then. He sucked in a deep breath, crouching down among the thick, tangled undergrowth, then slithered forward, eyes alert, trying to pick out the position of the other.

Far off he thought he heard the drumming of approaching horses and knew that this could be some of the other's friends riding up. If he stayed there the chances were that they would circle around him and take him from the rear while the first man kept him pinned down.

Pouching one of the Colts, he carefully parted the thorn bushes in front of him and peered through the opening, slitting his eyes, trying to catch an upward glance at the rim of the trail where the other had been a few moments before. He could see nothing there now, knew instinctively that the other had slipped away, was possibly much closer now and, with that rifle, would be able to stop him at a much greater distance than he could with only a revolver.

Taking off his hat, he balanced it on a short stick, pushed it up slowly, then pulled it down swiftly as the single shot rang out from less than a hundred yards away and a little to one side. There was a great hole drilled through the crown of the hat proving that the other was no mean marksman and that he had circled much further than Neil had anticipated.

Swinging around, he loosed off a couple of shots into the undergrowth. There followed no sound, and he guessed that neither of his bullets had found its mark.

Moving to one side, he began to circle himself, keeping to the right of the hidden marksman. His sorrel was standing a little distance away near a clump of trees. Careful as he was, the other must have heard the slight sound for more shots rang out and the fire sang though the trees, following him. He scuttled for one of the trees, flung himself down behind it, steadying himself. He knew now exactly where the other was, not too far away, certainly close enough to be reached by a revolver bullet. Still no sign of any more of these gunhawks. But he guessed that even then they were spurring their mounts forward as fast as they could ride, heading in the direction of the shooting.

Knowing the kind of man who had tried to shoot him down from ambush, Neil felt a cold wash of anger sweep through him, drowning out every other emotion in his mind, changing him, chilling him. Patience made rock out of him as he crouched there so that it seemed he could have waited for ever for the other to betray himself and make the wrong move. It was waiting that would break the other down, he felt sure of that.

Unfortunately, the other would also be aware that several of his friends were on their way, would arrive on the scene, too, and if he could keep Neil pinned down during that time, they stood a good chance of picking him off with little risk to themselves.

Somewhere, close at hand, he heard a horse begin to thresh, knew that it was not his own but that belonging to the man who had tried to kill him. He thinned his lips and grinned tightly in anticipation. At last he heard a sharp sigh come from the other as he let his breath go from between his lips. Swiftly Neil brought up his Colts in that direction, fired off a short volley into the brush, then went forward, slowly and cautiously, guns held ready. It had been that sudden need for air which had betrayed the other's presence, and the man seemed to have realised that almost instantly, for scarcely had the rolling echoes of Neil's shots died away than the other began to fire in his direction, shooting blindly and recklessly, without taking proper aim, hoping perhaps that if he fired a sufficient number of bullets, at least one of them was bound to find its mark.

Some part of his mind counted the other's shots, then he had plunged into the dense undergrowth, feeling the long thorny strands tug at his legs as he strode forward. He meant to make his man back away until he was forced to come out into the open space on top of the trail's rim, where the other had stood before when he had first opened fire. Once there, the bushwhacker would make a perfect target.

'You made a big mistake trying to gun me down, stranger,' he called softly, skipping to one side as the shot he had been expecting snapped through the air close to where his head had been a split second earlier. The other could not have many more slugs left in his rifle, would be forced to reload, unless he cared to rely on Colts. A pause, then Neil heard the other suddenly crashing through the brush as he turned on his heel and took to flight, back through the trees to where he must have tethered his mount.

He made out the scrape of the other's body through the tangled bushes, then caught a fragmentary glimpse of the gunman as he darted across an open patch of ground among the trees. Neil laid his gun along the running figure and squeezed the trigger gently, felt the Colt back against his wrist, saw the man fall forward on to his face and lie still.

Running forward, he went down beside the other, turned him over. The man was a stranger to him but he had the stamp of the gunhawk written all over his squat features. It hadn't been a long wait, but those other men would be close to the trail now, wouldn't have been wasting time getting to the scene of the shooting. He caught the bridle of his own mount, swung himself up swiftly into the saddle and rode out along the trail, crouching low in case there were any shots headed in his direction.

A spate of shots whistled past him as he rode. Then he had swung around a bend in the trail, was out of sight of the crowd of gunmen at his back. By the time he reached the stream most of the wagons were already over, the horses pulling them up the steep bank, rocking and swaying the Conestogas from side to side as they dragged them, dripping from the water.

The sun had risen now, was lying close to

the eastern horizon, big and red, full of the promise of more heat to come, but not yet with any real indication of the full heat which would develop around high noon.

Jackson came forward, looked at the dust that was heavy on Neil's jacket, where it caked his sweat-stained pants. Neil tilted his canteen to his lips, drank deeply.

'We heard shooting up there in the trees,' said the big man, speaking almost casually. 'Trouble?'

'Afraid so. There was one of those hombres waiting for me on top of the trail overhang among the trees. I reckon he's dead now, but several of his pals came riding up just as I got away. They'll be waiting for us in the brush.'

Jackson considered that, rubbing his flaming red beard, then he nodded ponderously.

'Reckon that since we know where they are, we might as well get moving.' He lifted a hand to halt the onward moving wagons for a moment. 'What would your advice be? Stay here and try to fight 'em off if they decided to rush us at the stream?'

'Depends on the men in the wagons, if they're willing to fight. Can they be trusted to handle their guns?'

'I reckon so. Don't worry none on that score. They'll fight.' A huge hand dropped on to Neil's shoulder as he slid from the saddle. The other's laugh was loud. 'I'll warn everybody what to expect, tell the women and kids to keep inside the wagons, and to stay down. That canvas won't stop a bullet.'

It was a blunt speech, but then Jackson was a blunt man. Neil waited while the other strode along the line of wagons, speaking to the men seated on each, saw the women and children move inside, saw the men reach out and loosen the long-barrelled Winchesters from their scabbards, check that they were loaded and ready for use. Jackson came back, taking a long-bladed knife from its leather sheath. He tested the edge with his thumb, balanced it carefully in the palm of his hand for a moment, his face dark. Then he glanced up sharply, his lips twisted into a vicious grin that was almost a snarl, showing the square teeth.

'Right, Roberts. Let's go!'

A wave of the huge right arm, then the wagons began to roll forward, away from the stream, wheels and axles creaking, the canvas tops shaking and swaying from side to side as they moved over the rough, stony ground, climbing up to the tall trees that dotted the earth on either side of the trail.

In among the trees were huge, massive

boulders which hung over the trail. Neil had spotted these on his ride out that morning, could guess where the killers would make their attack. It was possible that they would not be expecting the wagons to roll into the trees now that he knew that they were there, and the gunhawks would be debating whether to move down to the stream and attack them there. On either side of the slow-moving train rode grim-faced men on horseback, the outriders, their Colts in their hands, eyes flicking from side to side, alert for trouble, ready to meet it no matter from which direction it came.

The column had formed, the leading wagon reached the top of the stony rise and moved for the trees. Neil could feel the tenseness rising in him now, could sense the tightening of the muscles of his arms and chest. He switched his gaze from side to side, looking for the first glint of sunlight on the shiny steel of a rifle barrel that would give away the position of the waiting gunmen.

There was the feel of eyes watching their every move. Jackson motioned to the riders to swing forward. No point in taking too many chances if they were to get through without too many casualties.

Neil spurred his stud forward, heels

kicking into the horse's flanks. He was followed by Tom Jessup and the other men of the outrider team. A gun flared among the rocks, half-hidden by the fringe of trees. The harsh, flat sound bucketed in the clinging stillness that lay over everything, breaking over the rumble of the horses and the wagons. One of the riders close by suddenly clutched at his shoulder where a red stain began to bubble through the cloth of his shirt, dribbling between his fingers. He swayed in the saddle, managed to stay upright, dropping back towards the wagons.

More shots bucketed out of the rocks. Neil narrowed his eyes, swung the sorrel round sharply, brought up his Colt and loosed off a couple of swiftly sighted shots, saw a dark figure hidden in a cleft among the boulders suddenly throw up its arms and pitch forward, sliding down the smooth face of the rocks to land on a narrow ledge some ten feet above the trail.

Fanning out around the rim of the wagon train, the other riders joined in, racing past the slow-moving horses that hauled the Conestogas, heading for the bend in the trail where the shooting was coming from. A bullet drummed over Neil's head as he crouched low over the neck of the sorrel.

Then he reached a spot less than five feet from the trail's edge, flung himself down out of the saddle, and moved swiftly into the trees, pushing his way forward through the tangled brush and scrub. The other men were slipping from their mounts, urged on by Jackson.

One of the gunhawks lifted his head, tried to bring up his rifle to line it up on Neil's chest, then collapsed backward as the other's bullet found its mark. Behind them, the men in the wagons were firing too, adding the weight of their rifle fire to the sharper, more frequent sounds of the Colts.

Neil sank to the ground, flattened himself under a clump of mesquite, mindless of the tough bare branches that scratched and raked his face. He kept angling towards the left, detouring to get the extra cover, edging around the boulders among which the gunmen were hiding. When he was sure he had moved far enough to get around to the rear of them, he turned back, edging down the steep slope that overlooked the trail. Using what concealment the mesquite bushes afforded, he worked his way cautiously down the slope. The roar of the guns was a vast sound in his ears and occasionally a slug would tunnel through the branches around him and bury itself in the ground close to his body. Coming downslope into the deserted area to the rear of the boulders, he moved more carefully now, crawling forward an inch at a time, keeping his head low, judging the position of the gunslingers from the volume of their fire. Nearby a horse snickered and he froze instantly, keeping his body pressed tight towards the earth, listening for the faintest warning sound from dead ahead of him, which would tell him that the horse had given him away.

It came so suddenly, so close to him, far closer than he had imagined, that his taut nerves vibrated like plucked strings.

'Keep firing at those wagons, damn you! The rest of us will take care of those men in the trees.'

Neil sank to the ground, checked his guns. For a moment he lay quite motionless, his scalp still tingling at the narrow margin by which he had escaped blundering into the others. They were less than two feet away, directly below him, and now his straining ears picked out tiny sounds. A grunt and a low curse as some of the rifle fire from the wagons hummed and ricocheted off the boulders.

Cautiously, he began to ease his way

forward, snakelike, through the tall coarse grass that grew at the top of the rocky incline. A kind of haze formed in front of his eyes as he held his breath, then risked a quick glance over the top of the rocks. The whining scream of a ricochet, fired from the wagons, screeched past him less than a foot away, but he ignored it. There were seven men directly below him, and one man stretched out full length on the rocks to the right. One glance was enough to tell him that there was nothing to fear from this man, he had been caught by the fire from below.

Very carefully he got to his feet, saw the men at the wagons lower their rifles as they spotted him, outlined in the harsh glare of the sunlight. For a moment he noticed the outlaws directly below him pause, obviously puzzled by the sudden cessation of firing from the train. Then one of them, more sharp-witted than the others, turned his head swiftly, then relaxed imperceptibly as he saw the twin Colts levelled at him.

'Jest turn around slow and easy,' Neil advised. 'I don't want to have to shoot any of you in the back, but I will if you make me.'

Slowly the men turned to look down the barrels of the guns Neil held at his sides.

The barrels were still; stone steady. No use for any of the men to take the gamble and hope to outshoot him, but for an instant the thought crossed the mind of one of the men, lived briefly in his eyes. Then he shrugged, tossed his gun on to the rocks as the others did likewise.

'That's better.' Neil went down into the level patch among the rocks. Already the other men from the train were moving in, their rifles held steady on the gunslingers, covering their every move. Three of the men had been wounded and stood clutching their shoulders; one man badly hit, a film of whiteness under the leather of his face, the blood bubbling through his fingers with every breath that he took. He stood swaying against the tall rocks, strength and life bubbling out through the deep wound.

Keeping them covered, Neil called down to Clem Jackson, and the giant of a man came climbing upward, moving with an agility that belied his tremendous size.

'What do we do with them, Roberts?' he grated. 'I never was one for shooting down men in cold blood, although I doubt if that goes for these *hombres*.'

Neil eyed the six men casually, saw the look of fear that showed in one man's eyes.

'You wouldn't do it,' muttered one of the men sullenly. 'Three of us are in bad shape. We're through. You wouldn't shoot now?'

'You tried to gun down helpless women and children in those wagons down there,' said Neil softly. There was an overtone of menace in his voice.

'We only carried out our orders,' said another of the gunslingers.

'Whose orders?'

Sullenly again: 'Jesse Sherman's.'

'We figured that. Any reason why he should send *hombres* like you out to kill innocent women and children?'

'This is his land, my friend,' said one of the wounded men with a snarl. 'He don't allow any wagon trains to move over it.'

'I understood that the Government were turning over most of the land to the settlers,' murmured Neil quietly. He snapped his gaze from one man to the next.

'He reckons that he bought it ten years ago. We can't argue that point with him. Besides, he's a big man in these parts. We're only paid to carry out his orders, and if he says we're to run any wagon trains off his spread, that's what we gotta do.'

'Reckon that if we had any sense, we'd shoot the lot of you. Rattlers like you don't deserve to go on living.'

'They'll ride back to the ranch and warn Sherman of what has happened if we let them go,' said Jessup harshly. He held his rifle warningly in his hands, his finger crooked tightly around the trigger.

'It's a mighty long way to the ranch from here, best part of five days' journey on foot.'

'You ain't going to–' started one of the men, then fell silent as Neil swung his gun once more to line the barrel up on his chest, stopping all further argument.

'Better check where they left their horses, set 'em loose. These *hombres* can walk home. I reckon they'll be footsore by the time they get back to Sherman's ranch.'

'But Simms, Carter and Sneddon are wounded, they need a doctor fast,' argued one of the men. He slitted his eyes, starting forward.

Tension crackled in the heat that lay over the trees, flowing though the branches, over the tumbled rocks. Neil's eyes were bright with challenge, hands rigid around the guns, fingers crooked over the triggers, ready. Another step by the gunhawk would have started those guns hammering. Anything or nothing if the tension lasted another ten seconds. Then the other stopped, stepped back, face sullen, lips twisted with hate.

'That's better,' nodded Neil tightly. 'Didn't reckon you were such a damned fool as that.'

'You're goin' to regret this, mister,' growled the other harshly, the voice rasping from the depths of his chest. 'One of these days we're going to meet again, and the next time you won't have the drop on me. Then I'm going to kill you.'

'Maybe you'll get that chance,' grunted Neil. He lifted his gaze a fraction of an inch, saw the big man climbing over the rocks, searching for the horses. A moment later he heard Jackson's loud yell, followed by the stampeding thunder of hooves as the gunmen's mounts galloped from out of the trees, down the slope and across the plain. Jackson came back, gave a brusque nod.

'Reckon they won't be roundin' up those mounts in a hurry,' he said in a satisfied tone. 'You figgering on letting em go now?'

Neil nodded slowly. 'I guess so.' He turned to the others. 'Take your friends with you and get moving.'

It was simply said, but the words carried the promise of death if there was the slightest argument on the others' part. There was none. The gunslingers recognised the threat in the veiled tone. Slowly they made their way down through the rocks and boulders and into the trees. While the men from the wagons retrieved the guns which the gunhawks had discarded, Neil went back to his horse and mounted up. The wagons began to roll, bumping and swaying along the narrow trail between the tall trees. The timber was old first-growth pine, thick and massive at the butt, tapering in a smooth and flawless line towards the interwoven top covering which here made an almost solid umbrella against the sunlight. But if it kept out the light, it did not keep out the heat, and very soon sweat formed a film on his features, running down into his eyes and along his neck.

Far away he heard one solitary starved echo, a sharp blast of sound that might have been a gunshot, but he could not be sure, and it was not repeated. The tall, red-barked trees ran solemnly before them and somewhere over the thick arch of tangled boughs the noon sun blazed like an inferno fire, hidden by the green of the leaves, but here, under the trees, the air was blue-shadowed and still, with the hot smell of the pine needles in his nostrils. They broke cover by early afternoon, came out into the vast green plain that stretched away to the west. Far in the distance the cattle grazed, placid as yet, but how they might react to the wagons as they approached was something no man could have predicted, and there might be riders with the herd who would cause more trouble.

They held to the curve of the high ridge for as long at possible before dropping to the plain, heading west towards the distant herd on the shoulder of the low hills. Back of them, the mountains lifted to the unsullied arch of the heavens. Overhead the sun was lowering, westering, keeping its heat. Now that they were out in the open the heat struck them more forcibly than when they had been among the trees.

The wagons moved in single file, rumbling out of the trees at Neil's back as he sat the sorrel, pausing to turn and look behind him, running his gaze over the line of Conestogas. Ahead of them the sunlight shone on sleek backs and waving horns that caught and reflected the sunlight like polished slivers of glass. Around them now was a silence that was so deep and heavy and still that it seemed easy for a man to be able to reach out and touch it. A silence that was enhanced, rather than diminished, by the faint creak of the wagons as the horses plodded slowly over the soft earth and grass. Neil gigged his mount, rode in a great circle around the train, pausing to warn each of the outriders in turn of trouble. He had the feeling that it would come very soon, but from which direction he was not sure. Perhaps from that vast herd which they would soon pass, perhaps from the men who might be riding it, perhaps, although he did not think it likely, from the men they had left behind among the trees, left to walk back to the ranch or their nearest companions.

A quarter mile. Half a mile, and now they were well into the plain, moving out and away from the ridge at their backs. For a long while they rode in silence, men and women engrossed in their own thoughts, remembering the firing back along the trail, thinking how easy it would have been for some of them to have been lying back there with bullets in their bodies, looking ahead even to try to visualise what might lie in store for them, some eyeing the herd that moved like a rippling black wave over the side of the hill.

'We'll have to keep riding until we're clear of that herd,' Neil told Jackson, as he rode alongside the lead wagon, turning his head a little to eye the other. 'They look mean, could be trouble if we tried to camp too close. Besides, they'll have riders out fanning around them, especially after dark. Reckon they'll be just as mean as those critters we met back on the trail.'

Jackson nodded musingly. 'The horses are tired,' he observed. 'You reckon it would be wise to push them too far?'

'We've got to.' He knew it sounded hard, but there was no other choice open to them.

'If you say so.' Jackson flicked the long whip over the horses. The other wagons followed. Neil threw a swift glance at the sky. Another four, perhaps five, hours of daylight left. Then it would be dark, but they would have to keep the wagons moving that night, long after nightfall. Deliberately he edged the train away to the left of the herd, hoping to pass more than two miles from it. Perhaps he was being over cautious, seeing danger where none existed. It was not likely that Sherman would send out his paid killers to watch a herd, even one of that size. He could usefully employ them on better business. The men riding the perimeter of the herd would be ordinary cattlemen, skilled in the way of handling cattle, but not equally skilled in the ways of handling guns.

If he was right in this, there might be little danger. If he was wrong, then all hell might be let loose on the plain, a hell that moved on four feet, that held needle-sharp horns, a squat, evil head, and a ton or so of solid beef and muscle behind it. There was an odd edge of tension to his body as he sat the saddle, pushing his mount forward, eyes flicking from the wagon to the herd, and back again.

4

Stampede!

Slim Farrel had a dark, saturnine face, dominated by a thick black moustache and dark brows which slashed across his features like a black line drawn by some artist's swift stroke of the brush. His shoulders were broad and he had a deep, powerful chest but thin, spindly legs which looked as if they could scarcely support his own weight. He was a cattleman who had herded cattle across most of the vast continent until he had grown tired of the business and thrown in his lot with the wagon train, seeking fresh horizons to the west, further along the trail than he had ever travelled before, hoping to settle down in California. He now drove one of the wagons with the train, a man who kept himself to himself and did little talking along the trail.

Now, however, he had quite a lot to say. The wagon train was camped on a stretch of level ground by a narrow river that ran along the perimeter of the grasslands. Neil had set a hard pace. It had been an unwelcome decision, but an extremely necessary one. Not until they had left that herd behind was he satisfied that there was little danger to the train. They had seen nothing of Sherman's men with the herd, but there was the feeling that they had been watched all the way across the plain.

'Likely you're wonderin' why I insisted on making you travel so fast and hard this afternoon and evening,' muttered Neil.

'You scared of that herd back there?' queried Jessup. He raised his brows into a straight interrogatory line.

'Could be. Sherman knows we're here, I've had that feeling for a long while ever since we crossed the stream this morning.'

'If he wants to kill us, there's one sure way he can do it,' put in Farrel. His sharp blue eyes peered through the darkness, brows furrowed. There were years of knowledge in his brain, knowledge of cattle, their little meannesses and ways.

'Just what do you mean, old-timer?' asked Jessup. His eyes held Farrel's.

'That herd back there. It wouldn't take much to start them on the prod, set them stampeding in this direction. I'm a Texan. I've ridden herd more times than I care to remember. I've seen 'em at their best and at their worst. And I didn't like the look of that herd back there.'

'And you figger that's what they mean to do?' murmured Jessup. He seemed to be thinking over the possibility in his mind, as if the thought had never occurred to him before.

Farrel shrugged. 'I don't claim to read the minds of Sherman's men, but if I wanted to get rid of a wagon train and I had that damned great herd poised back there, just ready to move, I'd know just what to do.'

Jessup rapped his knuckles irritably against the pommel of the saddle lying on the ground close beside him. His strong teeth tore a strip of beef from the bone in his hands and he stretched one leg to ease the ache of his muscles. 'If they do decide to do that, this ain't the best place for the wagons to be.' A breath whistled in and out of his flared nostrils.

Around the fire nearby there was the murmur of voices. The others were preparing to settle down for the night. The children had been put to bed in the wagons and quietness was settling over the camp. The fire crackled and there was movement in the dark shadows that moved beyond the flickering glow of the fire.

'I'll check the horses,' muttered Jackson harshly. He got heavily to his feet and moved away from the fire.

Jessup waited until he had gone, then said softly: 'I don't like this, Roberts. A stampede is something I never bargained with when I said I'd make this drive, and I'm sure that goes for most of the others, too. A gunman I can stand up to and fight, but a thousand head of beef cattle on the run – that's something different. We wouldn't stand a chance against them. They'd run down the train and leave nothing once they'd passed over us.'

He turned to Farrel. 'You reckon that could happen? You know these steers. Would they start a stampede?'

'It only needs somebody to fire off a handful of shots in their ears and they'll start to run. They're damned funny, unpredictable creatures at the best of times. A thunderstorm could blow up and the heavens open with the sound of all hell being let loose, and they won't stir an inch. Then loose off one shot and they'll start and nothing will stop 'em.'

Jessup looked in doubt into the darkness. There was a sharp tenseness in his body. A moment later Jackson came back. 'Nothing moving out there. The horses seem skittish, though. Something worrying 'em. They can sense something.'

He looked in doubt towards Farrel. The darkness was sharpened by the bright pin-points of the stars glittering in the jet cloth of the heavens. Outside the camp there seemed to be a tremendous loneliness crouching there – a deep and tense loneliness which must have been a common thing to man right at the beginning of the world when these plains were first made. A fear-filled loneliness that ate at the nerves until they were drawn tight through the limbs.

Gradually the fire went down, leaving only glowing embers that pulsed with brief flashes of orange flames whenever the air caught at them, fanning them into bright-ness. The men and women in the wagons slept. The night air held a sudden chill. In his blanket within a few feet of the dying fire, Neil slept and not far away the horses dropped their heads. Perhaps two hours passed, then another. The moon lifted from the eastern horizon and threw a pale wash of yellow light over the scene. Inside his blanket, Neil stirred, then came fully awake, sitting bolt upright on the cold, hard ground, straining with every sense to pick up the sound which had woken him. For several seconds he sat there, peering into the moonlit darkness which lay around him.

Moments passed and still he could hear nothing. But something had woken him. There was no doubt about that. This was a feeling he had experienced many times before in the past and every time there had been something definitely wrong, and he knew it would be foolish to ignore it. Beside the fire he could make out the sleeping forms of Jackson and Jessup. Had he been mistaken? Was it just one of the ordinary sounds of the night which had woken him. Perhaps one of the horses snickering in the near distance on the edge of the camp – a log falling into the heart of the fire?

The slight sensation of apprehension in the pit of his stomach eased. He stretched a cramped leg forward to ease the tightening of the muscle of his hip. Then the sound came again and he was on his feet in an instant, head turning to the east from whence the sound came. A cattleman himself, he recognised it at once. A moment later he was shaking Jessup and Farrel awake, then moving over to where Jackson lay under his blanket.

'*Stampede!*'

Farrel yelled the single word at the top of his voice. A moment later he had fired a couple of wild shots into the air, the sharp, cracking echoes heard all over the camp. For most of the men in the wagons there was no need for warning.

Those who did not know from their own past experience could guess only too well what stampeding cattle meant. Countless tons of solid beef and muscle on the move, slashing horns and lowered squat heads. All of the meanness that could be found anywhere on God's earth rolled into one vast avalanche of lunging and bellowing, fear-crazed beasts. The herd could only have been three miles away, and yet even from that distance it was possible to hear it crashing into action, the ground beginning to shake. Neil leapt for his horse, swung the saddle up and tightened the cinch with swift movements of long practised hands. Then he was up in the saddle, Jessup and Farrel beside him.

Leaning down, he yelled to Jackson as the big man moved towards his own horse. 'We'll try to head 'em off. You'd better get into the lead wagon. Head them out of here. The ground's far too open. Get them across the stream and on to the other side. There's rough ground there a mile or so ahead. Try to make for that and get everybody into the lee of the hills.'

Jackson gave a quick, brusque nod of his great head to indicate that he had under-stood. He ran for the wagon, leaving his own horse to make its own way over the stream. Around the wagons themselves there was feverish activity. Fortunately everyone had heeded the warnings given by Farrel the night before and the horses were readily hitched into the shafts. All were awake by now. It was doubtful if anyone could have slept. Not after those twin bucketing shots from Farrel's gun and the growing thunder of the stampeding herd in the distance. Neil bent forward in the saddle, knees pressing tightly to keep his seat as the sorrel moved forward into the night. An animal trained for this type of work, the stud knew exactly what to do. Horse and rider became as one as he headed the sorrel away from the dying embers of the fire. Jessup and Farrel on either side of him, dark shadows in the pale yellow moonlight that washed over the plain, lighting on the sluggish water of the nearby river. But Neil had no eyes for that. The people in the wagons would have to make the best time they could and depend upon Clem Jackson to get them over the river and into what safety they could find on the other side. Certainly, so long as they remained where they were, they were in terrible danger. That stampeding herd would stop for nothing, and certainly the river would prove no barrier to their onward rush. It was doubtful if they would stop for the rocks up ahead.

Two other riders detached themselves from the train at Jackson's harshly yelled orders and galloped after Neil and his two companions. They rode loosely, reins hanging loose, their arms swinging, making no attempt to guide their mounts. Somewhere ahead of them came a tidal wave of tossing horns, heads, hooves and tons of muscle. Neil felt the tightness growing in his chest. Dimly, over the thunder of the stampede, he heard the sharp barks of guns blazing, knew then, even if he had only suspected it before, that the herders with those cattle had deliberately started the steers on the run, knowing that they would trample down the wagon train where it was camped on the river's edge. He tried to push his gaze ahead of him, to pick out the black surge of the herd as it came forward. In the moonlight, shadows were tantalising things, not once materialising so that he could see things clearly and properly. He reached the tip of a low rise, reined his mount, lifting his right hand to check the onward rush of the four riders with him. His feet found the stirrups as he paused there, peering directly ahead of him.

'There!' Jessup yelled the word savagely, pointed a finger into the darkness.

Neil narrowed his eyes, looked in the direction of the other's pointed finger, then sucked in his breath sharply, felt the muscles under his ribs tighten convulsively. No time to look about them now. No time even to try to think. That vast sea of dark shadow was already streaming over the plain, heading in their direction. He did not doubt that the stud he rode could quarter across the face of the rushing herd and still outrun it. But there were the wagons at his back to think of. Somehow they had to try to turn the tip of the herd, to divert them from the path they had already chosen, turn them around and try to send them plunging along the bank of the river, heading them south. If they could do that then they stood a good chance of saving all of the wagons. If not–

He did not allow himself to think of the consequences of failure. He had seen too many herds stampeding not to know what happened to anything that was unfortunate enough to get into their path.

A swift glance behind him and he saw to his relief that the wagons were just beginning to get under way. The first had moved down into the water, was crossing the river. But he knew instinctively that they could never make it in time unless the herd were turned. Any chance of stopping those animals had gone the moment those gunshots had been fired behind them. Strange and moody, utterly unpredictable, they had begun to move.

No time to worry about the wagons now. Swiftly he pulled the Colt from its holster, gigged the mount. It leapt forward, down the far side of the slope, down towards the thundering mass of the herd. Beside him rode the other men. If there was any fear in their minds at what they saw directly ahead of them, nothing of it showed in their actions. There was no hesitation now on their part. Swiftly Neil swung the sorrel so that it was racing across the edge of the herd, while with his left hand he gestured to the men with him to swing around, to follow his lead in everything he did. Success or failure, life or death depended on split second timing here. One false move on their part and they could be trampled down by that sea of horns. Lunging and bellowing the herd came on. The riders with them were far to the rear. They had started the fear-crazed beasts on their way and were now hanging back, keeping themselves out of danger.

Jessup rode swiftly, cutting towards the side of the herd. His gun was out and he fired savagely, straight into the faces of the animals alongside him. Above the thunder of the thousands of hooves it was impossible to make out any other sound. Neil reached the tip of the crescent, where the foremost steers formed a vast bulge, racing ahead of the drag. Behind them came the mass of the herd, following blindly on the heels of the leaders. If only they could turn the steers that led the herd they might stand a chance. The thought pounded on and on through Neil's mind as he headed the sorrel straight for the fanning group, his gun spitting flashes of orange flame into the eyes of the beasts close to him, seeking to crowd them over to the right, to divert them from the path they were taking.

But it was as if the devil had got into them that night. They were being driven on by the fear of the guns which had roared behind them, startling them, setting them running, out across the open face of the plain, out towards the river. No barrier there as far as they were concerned. Again and again the other men were firing and loading, clinging to the backs of the bucking horses with tightened knees. It was mean and cruel work. Dropping a steer here and there in the hope of forcing them to change their course, to set them swinging in a wide arc. Jessup slashed at the faces of the charging, plunging steers with his coiled riata once his guns were empty, yelling harshly and savagely at the top of his voice. Nearer at hand, Farrel, old to this game, continued to thrust his mount against the bulging side of the herd, adding the fire from his guns to the din.

Gradually, as the minutes passed, there was a wave forming along the length of the herd. But a swift glance told Neil that it would be too late. They could not hope to hold them, even to turn them completely along the nearer bank of the river.

A bunch split out from the main herd, went careering out across the dark plain, just visible in the flooding moonlight as they raced away, bellowing and lowing in anger and fear. Neil watched them for the briefest fraction of a second, then let them go, turning his glance back to the others. There was no danger from that small bunch. They would go on running until they stopped from sheer exhaustion and by that time they would be miles away from there. He doubted if they would cross the river. It was the big body of cattle that worried him.

Now they were less than half a mile from the river bank. A quarter of an hour was gone, a period made up of minutes which had ticked themselves away into a roaring, bellowing thunderous eternity. The mad eyes of the steers could be seen in the shadows of the shaggy heads. The horses were doing their best, the guns were still flaring at the crazed beasts, but it was making little difference.

Turning his mount, Neil rode swiftly for the river. Behind him the roaring herd came full pelt across the plains. Somehow he had to reach the wagons and try to get them under cover. Not that he doubted Clem Jackson's ability to do the best he could. But

114

the other lacked his experience of this country, did not know it as he did. All hell couldn't stop that herd now. He hit the water at the run, felt the current crash against the sorrel's chest as it began to move over.

For a moment the horse lost its footing on the smooth bed of the river, on the stony bed, went floundering forward, its neck arched, almost under. Then, with a tremendous effort, it found its feet again, righted itself, crashed on until it reached the opposite bank, plunged up it into the rocky, rough ground that lay beyond. The last of the wagons was on the trail on the far side, rocking and swaying from side to side as the horses plunged and heaved on the traces. How long those wagons would take that kind of punishment he did not know. But it needed only one of them to break down now, and it would be impossible to save it from the death that came close behind, a surging, terrible sea of death.

Water dripping from his pants, he clung to the back of his stud, raced it along the trail after the wagons. Fifty yards, a hundred. By now, he thought, not turning to see, the herd must have reached the river. Jessup and the others would have reached it, too, would be doing their best to turn it. The river was the last obstacle in the way of the stampede. If they did not manage to turn it there, they had no chance in hell of doing it anywhere else.

Half a mile away lay the craggy hills. There lay the only safety they could find. The lead wagon was almost there, but the others were strung out over more than a quarter of a mile, dashing forward as hard as they could go, the men and women in those lurching, swaying Conestogas knowing full well what would happen to them if they stopped now, if they didn't make the rocks. Behind him, breathing down the back of his neck, the herd came on, closer and closer with every passing second. A swift glance over his shoulder and he saw that the leaders were over the river, that the others were in the swim. His heart sank within him and he groaned aloud as he saw the danger. The men were riding close to the plunging, snorting animals, still firing their guns in their faces, still hoping to cut them over the plain to the south. He knew that they had very little chance. The distance was so small that the leading steers would be upon the last wagons before they reached safety.

Guns were spreading death among the plunging, roaring steers. But there was a limit to what a handful of guns could do. That limit had been reached.

Drilling his spurs into the flanks of his sorrel, he sent it racing along the dark trail, knowing that the slightest slip could mean the end for him. But the sorrel was a sure-footed creature, picked its way easily through the boulders which lay scattered over the trail. As he rode he peered ahead, trying to pick out the shapes of the wagons clearly. Too close ahead, they were moving too slowly. He sucked in a deep breath, pondered his next move. He knew that Jackson had understood everything he had told him, knew that the other would do all that he could to get the train under cover of the rocks. But the horses were tired, the wagons were cumbersome things, and it was dangerous to try to drive them as hard as this. Over the smooth ground of the desert to the east they might have got away with it, but here on this rough, stony ground disaster was always very close.

It came with the suddenness of a bolt of lightning. Not the last wagon, but the one immediately in front of it. One minute it was on the trail, racing forward, the canvas top shuddering, the wheels churning in the rocks. The next it had plunged sideways as if

117

a giant had struck it, hurling it to one side.

Neil forced a sharp groan through tightly clenched teeth. One of the rear wheels had split, must have hit a boulder the wrong way and, at that speed, the shattering force of the impact had been more than enough to smash the wheel to pieces. The end of the wooden axle was digging deep into the hard ground, scraping forward as the horses continued to pull on the traces. Another few yards and it would go over. But before that could happen the frantically struggling horses succeeded in snapping the leather of the traces, and the team ran free, surging forward into the darkness. The wagon turned sharply at right angles and came to rest across the trail. Savagely, Neil urged his mount forward. Out of the corner of his eye he saw the black mass of the herd over to his left. They had crossed the river back there and were running free and wild over the rough terrain here. They were no longer on to the trail but swinging over the ground to his left, directly on to the smashed wagon. He knew with a sick certainty that there was nothing he could do to prevent them from getting there before he did. They were sweeping forward now in an irresistible wave. Somehow he got the sorrel alongside the leaders, turning his Colt on them, firing savagely and blindly into their faces. Even at that last moment he had the feeling that it might have been possible for him to turn them just that necessary fraction so that the black tide might swing past the wrecked wagon. The last wagon in the train had somehow pulled clear, had gone bucking and swaying past, although it was still in terrible danger. Steers went down before his flaming guns, but there were always others to move forward and take their places, trampling down those which had been killed. Another shot, a vivid splash of orange flame and a steer dropped dead. Swiftly he tried to bulwark the smashed wagon by building a wall of dead steers in front of it, a dam of flesh and bones and curving horns to keep away the cattle which came behind.

The man who had been driving the wagon had been tossed out when the wheel had gone. He lay on the trail a couple of yards away, face downward, his arms and legs out flung. He did not move, and it was impossible to tell whether he had been killed outright by the fall or whether he had simply been knocked cold. Aiming with an almost unconscious movement, Neil dropped two steers next to the fallen man, but it was no use trying to form a barrier there. The dark wave descended on them and the figure of the man lying in the dust was blotted out in a massacre of stamping hooves.

The wagon itself lay directly in the path of the crazed animals. As he drew alongside he debated whether to clamber on board and risk his life doing so, or whether to try to mill the herd about him. A moment while he slashed at bawling, lunging heads, their wicked, needle-sharp horns missing his legs and thighs by inches. Then the wet folds of the canvas collapsed as the tremendous weight of the herd surged over it. Wood split and splintered under that massive onslaught. He thought he heard a woman scream, a thin lost sound in the night. But he could not be certain in that bellowing, savage roar that filled the whole of creation.

Turning the sorrel, he pulled it into the side of the trail. The rest of the herd thundered by, dust rising from their pounding hooves, choking and clogging at the back of his throat and nostrils. His eyes were filled with grit and it was almost impossible to see anything. Certainly he could hear nothing but the sound of that stampeding herd roaring past him. The body of a steer slid against the sorrel, threatening to crush it against the solid rock face nearby. Deftly Neil clung to the saddle, kept his hands tight on the reins. No point in trying to drop any more of the animals. The damage had been done. All he could hope for now was that Jackson had got the other wagons into some kind of safety, some refuge from the black avalanche which threatened to roll over them all and annihilate them utterly.

There were suddenly more shouts in the night. Jessup and Farrel and the others, moving forward along the curving side of the herd where it bulged as it was fed by the mass of animals crushing forward from behind. As the herd curved away from him, Neil urged his stud forward, away from the sheer rock face at his back.

'Hiiiya! Hiii-ya! Git over... Git over!' The shrill cries echoed in his ears as the rest of the men surged along by him. They must have known that now there was nothing more they could do. The herd would continue along the trail until they were exhausted, when they would stop. If the wagons were not under cover now, then they were finished and nothing in heaven or on earth could save them.

As the minutes passed there came a lessening in the crash of the herd as the last of the stragglers went by. The guns stopped their hammering roar. No point now in continuing to fire. If they hadn't got the leaders, the rear would never change their onward rush. Once the herd had moved by, he made himself go forward to where the smashed and splintered remains of the wagon still lay in the middle of the trail. It was now something virtually unrecognisable. The canvas had been torn to shreds that fluttered in the breeze, and the wooden upright had been splintered and crushed, the wheels torn from the axles and ground into the dirt. Yet there was still someone alive in there. Neil heard the low groan quite distinctly, although a second fled before his mind accepted the fact that everyone had not been killed outright. It seemed inconceivable to him that anyone could have lived through that pounding rush but–

Within seconds he had slid from the saddle, was yelling at Farrel to join him. His hands tore with a desperate urgency at the sodden canvas strips that covered the debris. Blinking his eyes, he tried to see in the gloom. Farrel dropped to the ground a couple of yards away, came running forward, gave the trampled red thing in the middle of the trail only a cursory glance. Then he was on one knee beside Neil, tugging at the weight of the splintered wagon.

'Reckon there's somebody trapped inside there – still alive,' muttered Neil harshly. 'Heard 'em cry out a moment ago.'

'Hell, they can't be unhurt,' said the other. He shook his head slowly, wonderingly.

Neil knew what was in the cattleman's mind. Under that stamping wall of bone and muscle, nothing could have escaped unscathed. He pulled hard at wood and metal. The groan came again and he was able to locate the sound in the darkness. Then his outstretched hand touched a woman's head. She moaned and sucked in her breath hard. His fingers drifted over her shoulders then down to her arm, and he felt the shudder pass through her at his touch.

'She's here, Farrel,' he said tightly. 'I think her arm is broken. It may be trapped under the beam. Better try to lift it. Careful now!'

Together they lifted the heavy beam which pinned the woman's arm down. She uttered another loud moan, then was silent. Neil bent, listened for a moment, then nodded as he heard the harsh whistle of air rasping in and out of her lungs. She had fainted. In the circumstances that was perhaps the best thing that could have happened. Now at

123

least she would feel nothing when they came to move her.

Carefully they managed to free her, to lift her clear of the wagon. In the dull wash of yellow moonlight, Neil recognised her. Claire Vance, riding with her husband to a new life in California. He felt a sharp tightening of his throat muscles. That would be Tom, her husband, lying out there among the rocks a few feet away. Whatever happened, she must not come round and see him.

'Let's get her away from here,' he said tightly, 'before she wants to know what happened to her husband.'

'What about kids?' asked Farrel harshly.

'None. Damned good thing, too. They'd have been killed in this mess.'

Carefully he lifted the woman on to his saddle, then led the sorrel along the trail to where the wagons had moved towards the rocks. The herd had gone, thundering onward in a straight line, in their blind, blundering rush which would carry them for many miles before they finally halted. At the back of his mind there was a sharpening sense of anger, a blinding thing, which urged him to deliver the woman to the train and then turn, ride back and try to hunt down those murderers who had started that stampede. But common sense told him that not only would those men have moved off into the darkness of the plain, but he would be needed more urgently at the wagon train.

They made slow progress along the rough trail and by the time they reached the rocks the train had begun to move back out into more open ground again. They had been lucky, fantastically so. Far luckier than he would have ever thought possible. Jackson had located the small side canyon halfway along the rocky path through the hills and had somehow succeeded in turning the train into it. Here they had been perfectly safe from the thundering hooves of the steers as they plunged past along the main trail. But there were a few steers scattered on the trail near the entrance to the small side canyon which told of a desperate fight to keep the crazed animas at bay and prevent them turning.

Clem Jackson stepped forward as Farrel rode up, then turned and eyed Neil curiously as he walked forward with the woman lying over the saddle. His thick black brows went up into a mutely questioning line over the dark eyes.

'She'll be all right once we've fixed her arm,' Neil told him quietly. 'At least I couldn't find any other bones broken. But the wagon was smashed completely and she's lucky to be alive.'

'What about Tom Vance?' boomed the other.

Neil shook his head slowly. 'At least he never knew what hit him. He was thrown from the wagon when it hit a boulder and split the wheel. He must have died at once. If he didn't, then he was unconscious by the time the herd got to him.'

'I'll get one of the women to look after her.' Jackson gave a quick nod, then reached up and lifted the woman down in his huge arms as if she were a baby and had no weight at all. He carried her into the rocks where the rest of the men and women were gathered. They had all had a shaking experience and it would be some time before they got over it, Neil reflected. But for Claire Vance, things would never be the same again. There would be no new life in California for her now. She would never even know what had happened to her husband, and for him there would be no proper grave. He felt a sudden weariness in him which was something more than the tiredness that came from the long night and the endless battle with that stampeding herd.

'One more piece of trouble like that and

the train will be finished before we've gone another fifty miles,' said Farrel. He built a smoke, stood quite still watching the rest of the folk sitting among the rocks, oblivious of the cold night air that blew about them. It was as if they could sense the tragedy of what had happened, knew that someone had died during the night, and for them, as for Claire Vance, it would never be quite the same again. They had seen death in one of its more terrible aspects, death in the form of a thundering, bawling wall of steers, something primitive and frightening, old to the cattlemen, but new to the others.

Neil sighed, dragged himself to his feet. There was stubble on his chin and the back of his hand rasped over it as he rubbed his face.

Jackson came back. He stood looking at the wagon nearby for a long moment, then said: 'We may have to rest up for tomorrow morning and carry out some repairs, Roberts. There'll be rims to be fitted to the wheels of some of the wagons, and fresh axles put on at least two of them before we go any further.'

'It might be best if we did rest up for the morning.' Neil nodded. 'I don't think there will be any further danger from the herd. By morning it will be miles away from here. But as for the men with it, that's a different matter. We'll need to be on our guard in case they try to attack us. I figure we may even get a visit from Sherman himself with some of his hired killers.'

'You know this man personally?'

'We've met before,' Neil admitted. 'The same goes for Hollard. I reckon those two are in cahoots now that they know we're moving across this stretch of country. They'll do anything in their power to stop us.'

Daybreak found them huddled around the fires. A cold wind had blown up after midnight and the clouds which had begun to gather, blotting out the yellow face of the moon, brought rain and discomfort. There was hot coffee in the boiler over the fire and they ate their breakfast hurriedly, before starting repairs to the wagons. The threat of danger still hung over them all. It was a tangible thing that could be felt and men had only to look up to where the two men were standing atop the tall columns of rock nearby to know that it might come at any moment.

Claire Vance was lying in one of the wagons, her arm fixed in a sling. Neil had climbed on board to take a look at her twice that morning, found her each time staring up at the sodden canvas over her head, her eyes open and wide, with only a vague emptiness in them. She neither turned nor seemed to hear him when he spoke to her and, after a few moments, he climbed down from the wagon into the pouring rain, and went back to the others.

'You figure she'll be all right, Roberts?' asked Jackson harshly, the second time he came back. 'I saw her a little while ago and she didn't seem to know I was there.'

'Shock,' said Neil briefly. 'It can do strange things at times. Maybe she still thinks that her husband is alive. Sooner or later she'll come out of it, and that will be the time when the pain will strike. I've seen it happen before. The mind pulls itself behind some dark curtain and shuts itself off from reality. As soon as we get away from here and that arm of hers heals a little, we'll get one of the women to break the news to her.'

Jackson nodded. They went back to work on the wagons fitting the new rims to the splintered wheels, checking the axles, the canvas and the traces. The rain continued to fall in a dark, hazy curtain from the heavens, so that there seemed no place where they could find dryness or comfort. Weary men who had been awake all night. Gaunt and haggard men who shook the rain from their hats and pulled their coats and jackets more tightly about their bodies as the cold wind blew down from the north, down from the distant mountains that loomed on the skyline, just a little closer now.

Shortly before noon one of the look-outs on the rocks yelled harshly. Neil glanced up at the man as he pointed to the west. Then he scrambled up the rocks to where the other stood, his gun whispering from its holster.

Ten riders had checked their mounts on a rise of ground to the west, men who looked out towards the hills. They seemed to be men who had ridden hard and ridden fast. The leader lifted a hand, urged the others forward again, and in that moment Neil recognised him. Jesse Sherman. There had been no mistaking that tall figure.

'Looks like trouble,' he said casually to the man standing by his side. 'I'll warn the others. You stay here and keep an eye on them.' He made his way down the rocky slope again, uneasy and apprehensive. For the moment he knew that these men did not intend to attack them. Had that been the case, they would have moved up unseen, keeping to the rocks and ravines which split the country in that direction.

'Sherman and some of his killers are headed this way,' he told Jackson. 'I doubt if they mean trouble just now,' he added, as the other reached for his Winchester. 'But I'm interested to know why they've come like this.'

Almost without direction, his hand loosed the gun in his holster. There was the sound of horses in the near distance, riding towards them, then the riders, bunched close together, came into view, Sherman leading them. He reined his mount a few yards away, stayed the men with him with a gesture of his hand. There was a sneer over the darkly handsome features as they stared down at Neil.

'Somehow, I figured it would be you, Roberts, leading this wagon train over my land.' There was a touch of menace in the other's cold voice. 'I reckoned we would meet again some day.'

'There ain't no law that says a man can't move over this stretch of country,' broke in Jackson in his loud, booming voice.

'I'm the law in these parts,' said Sherman tightly. 'All of this country that you can see, right to the horizons, belongs to me. If I say that you can't cross it, then the law backs me up. Could be you'd like me to send some of my men into Twin Creeks and get the sheriff out here.'

Neil grinned sardonically. 'There ain't much doubt in my mind, Sherman, that the sheriff there will do exactly as you tell him to. If he don't, then it won't be hard to replace him.'

'Just what are you insinuatin', Roberts?' snarled the other. For the moment his right hand hung poised over the gun at his hip, his eyes holding the promise of death in them.

'Just try it,' said Neil warningly. 'You'll be a dead man before you can get that gun clear of leather – and you know it. And if you're banking on one of your gunslingers getting me first, I reckon it might pay you to take a look around you. There are rifles pointed at every one of you and these men won't hesitate to shoot you down like the rattlers you all are. They ain't forgotten the way your men set that herd on to them last night. We lost a good man then, and there's a woman lying back there with a broken arm and her husband gone.

'These folk ain't asking much of anybody. Only the right to keep on moving until they get to California – and neither you, nor anybody else is going to stop 'em.'

He saw Sherman's gaze slide from side to side, saw the other stiffen a little and then drop his hand swiftly to his side as he saw the grim-visaged men who stood around the trail, the Winchesters and Colts rock-steady in their hands, their fingers bar-straight on the triggers. There was a long moment of silence on the trail. Close at hand a horse snickered, but that was the only sound that broke the clinging, heart-stopping stillness. It needed only one of the men with Sherman to make a wrong move to start those guns hammering, to fill the air with death.

With an effort Sherman forced himself to relax. A smile spread slowly over his features. 'I ain't going to forget this, Roberts,' he said softly, tonelessly, his voice oddly flat. 'I got a score to settle with you from way back and I intend to do it. You won't slip through my fingers this time as you did before. As for this wagon train, you're all fools if you believe this man and think that you will get through to California.'

'Your herd didn't finish us, and the same will go for your men if you try anything,' Jackson said harshly. 'We mean to ride through here to the mountains and you ain't going to stop us.'

'We'll see about that. If it's trouble you want, then by God you'll all get it. You'll begin to wish that you'd stayed back East where you were safe before I'm through with you.'

Before any of the others could speak, he had jerked the reins in his hands with a savage motion, wheeling his mount cruelly. He rode off along the narrow trail, the men following him. Slowly the thunder of their horses died into the distance and there was only the endless sound of the rain as it hit the hard rocks around them.

Neil drew in a deep breath and ran a dry tongue around equally dry lips. He stared at Jackson. 'I reckon we'd better get everything ready as quickly as we can and move out soon. I won't feel safe until we hit Twin Creeks. That's on the edge of Sherman's territory.'

'Reckon we can get supplies there?' asked Farrel. 'We're low on flour.'

'If we get through I reckon we can,' said Neil dully. He turned and went back to the waiting wagons. Throughout the rest of the morning and the long, grey, wet afternoon, they worked, ignoring the rain, the cold and the discomfort. The rain continued to fall endlessly, huge drops that soon turned the trail into a stretching river of mud. Overhead the clouds were low and thick, piling up from the western horizons in large masses. There had been no sign of the sun all that day, no sign of any let up in the rains. By late afternoon they were able to hitch up the horses and start the wagons rolling.

5

Twin Creeks

It was ten days later and nearly two hundred miles by the time the wagon train rolled into the township of Twin Creeks. In the hot dusty sunlight the town seemed asleep with the heat haze of high noon hanging over it. The wagons had stopped half a mile from the edge of the town and Neil and Jackson had ridden into the town to check on supplies. They reined their mounts at the end of the long street that stretched clear in front of them to where it moved all the way through the town and out the far side. The buildings had been erected on either side of that single street, stores and saloons, hotels and livery stables.

It was a town that was similar to hundreds of others in the west. A frontier town which pinpointed where the tide of civilisation, moving westward, had halted at some time in the recent past and men had set up a community here, to act as a bulwark against the Indians, who had ridden these plains long before the white man had come and wrested the land from them. Now, even though the white man had come, the place was still almost as wild as it had been in those early days when the frontier had stopped right there and there had been nothing beyond, to the west, but empty desert and unexplored mountains, herds of buffalo that roamed the plains in their millions.

The lie of the land on either side of Twin Creeks was of two different types. To the east stretched the rough country which merged gradually into the lush grasslands of the Sherman spread, with low rolling ridges that blended perfectly with the background. Westward lay the tall hills, a rugged country of rock and sharp-cut ravines, here pinnacles and boulders and buttes were all jumbled together, tumbling over each other as they lay spread out to join the tall mountains that spiked the horizon. The town lay in a wide hollow between these two strikingly opposite terrains, with the clear water of the two creeks that ran down from the hills to the west and gave the town its name, shining brilliantly in the hot sunlight.

Neil's eyes searched along the apparently deserted street for any sign of life. There were some. Men who sat on the boardwalks, in the shade of the single-storey buildings, their legs up on the wooden staging on the edge of the street, their hats pulled well down over their eyes. A handful of horses stood lazily in front of one of the saloons, tethered to the hitching post, their heads dropping in the sullen, oppressive heat.

Slowly the two men rode along the main street, eyes alert. It was not so much the look as the actual feel of possible danger that sent little warning currents surging through Neil's body. There was no doubt that they were exciting some curiosity from the people there. It was quite usual for folks to stare at him and he did not find it in the least disconcerting, but now he guessed that most of them were staring at the giant of a man who rode beside him, the hair and jutting beard making him look even more huge than he really was.

The wide brim of Neil's border hat

extended well from the crown on all sides, keeping the heat off his face and the glare of sunlight out of his eyes. He sat the sorrel quite relaxed, but although he scarcely seemed to move his head, it might have been noticed that his eyes were never still, that they flickered continually from side to side, taking in everything, missing nothing.

There was only one two-storey building in the whole town, the hotel which stood halfway along the street, a wide gallery around three sides of it. A tall man stood on the gallery, his legs spread wide as if bracing himself against some sudden lurch of the building which might pitch him down into the street below. He gave the two men a swiftly appraising glance, then turned sharply on his heel and vanished from sight. Probably, thought Neil tightly, going to warn someone of their arrival in town. There was bound to be someone anxious to know when they got there. Here, in Twin Creeks, it was possible that he would be recognised and he did not doubt that his name and reputation were well known to most of the people here.

He gigged his mount again, then motioned towards the nearby saloon. Jackson nodded, licked his lips, turned his mount, reined in, in front of the hitching rail. He slid easily from the saddle, then fell in with Neil as they went inside, away from the heat.

The saloon was almost deserted. A couple of men were seated at one of the tables near the windows. Four more were playing cards at the far end of the room, but that was all. Neil made his way towards the bar, eyed the bartender through narrowed eyes. He did not recognise the man, doubted if the other knew his identity, but the same might not go for any of the men at the tables.

'Whisky for both of us,' he said. 'Leave the bottle. It's thirsty work riding out there.'

The bartender brought the bottle up from beneath the bar, set it in front of Neil, then placed the couple of glasses beside it. His eyes were narrowed a little and he seemed plainly puzzled. 'You been riding the trail long?' he inquired.

'Long enough to work up a thirst,' Neil told him casually. He threw the whisky back. It burned his throat a little but washed some of the dry dust out of his mouth and sent a wave of warmth through his stomach. 'Where could we eat in this town?'

'If you ain't too particular about the food, I reckon I could fry you up something. Potatoes and beans and some bacon.'

'That'll go down fine,' said Jackson. He poured himself another drink and held the glass in his hands for a long moment staring down at the amber liquid in it. None of the men in the saloon had stirred since their entry, and Neil guessed that they had not recognised him, were not concerned with a couple of strangers who came riding into town.

'There's a room through the back if you'd care to go inside,' said the man behind the bar. 'I'll have the meal ready for you in ten minutes.'

They moved into the other room. There was a plate at one of the tables with a slice of steak on it, cut through in the middle, with a cup of coffee, half-finished, beside it, steam still rising from it. Neil eyed it sharply, but gave no sign to the bartender that he had noticed. Not until the other had pulled the heavy curtains back over the opening did he catch a tight hold of Jackson's wrist, motion him to silence, saying in a hoarse whisper:

'There's something wrong here. Somebody was inside this room a couple of minutes ago, must've seen us come in. He's slipped out now, whoever he was, maybe to warn the sheriff.'

'More of Sherman's work? You said that he ran this town – and the law here.'

'Could be. Maybe they figure that with us out of the way, the train won't be able to go on. Maybe they reckon it might turn back, or even stay here.'

He swung his eyes to the curtains over the entrance. A load of buckshot through there and it would mean the end of Jackson and himself. Swiftly he cast his eyes about for another way out, knew that there had to be one, because the man who had been in there a couple of minutes before had clearly slipped out without them seeing him. Then his gaze lit on the door at the far end of the room, a door almost completely hidden by the wooden cases that had been carefully piled in front of it. Very cleverly done, he thought, some of the anger beginning to rise in his stomach. His hands tightened savagely as he pushed back his chair and rose swiftly to his feet.

This play had been deliberately engineered by either Sherman or the sheriff here in Twin Creeks. By now they would be heading for the saloon. There would be some charge trumped up against Jackson and himself, and before they knew what had happened, they would find themselves locked up in the jail here. Then they would either be lynched by the mob, deliberately stirred up by Sherman, or shot in the back trying to make a break. Any chance they had of getting back to the waiting wagon train would be gone. He pressed his lips together into a hard, tight line across the middle of his features.

Outside, beyond the curtain that blocked off all sight of what was happening inside the saloon itself, he heard someone talking in a low voice. Then there were other voices, the sound of men moving into the saloon. Turning, he gave Jackson a quick glance full of meaning, saw the other reach down to check the guns in his holsters, then give a quick nod to indicate that he understood perfectly what was in Neil's mind. A second later Neil reached out and jerked the heavy curtain aside, stepping forward into the saloon.

There was a small knot of men just inside the door. He recognised Sherman, a curious expression on his face. Behind him was a short, stout man with a hard face and the star of a sheriff pinned to his shirt. Sherman was in the act of speaking to the sheriff when Neil moved into the room, eyes taking in every detail of the saloon, from the man in the white apron standing tensely at the back of the bar, to the two groups of men still seated at the tables. Even as his gaze flicked over them, they pushed back their chairs and moved away into the far corner of the room. Evidently these men were not part of the deal, wanted nothing of the gunfight which they sensed was in the offing, getting out of the line of fire.

'Looks to me as though you're trying to find somebody, Sherman,' said Neil, in a steady, even tone.

For a moment he saw that he had taken the rancher off his guard, that the other was a little unsure of himself, saw the flicker of uncertainty at the back of his eyes. Then Sherman nodded sharply, back on balance once more, dangerous, tricky. He said thinly: 'That's right, Roberts, I warned you back on the trail that you and the wagons you were leading were trespassing on my land. The sheriff here is to see that the law is carried out.'

'The law?' There was a note of deliberate sarcasm in Neil's tone now and he moved forward a couple of steps away from the heavy curtain, aware of the huge figure of Jackson at his back.

'That's right.' The portly figure of the sheriff stepped forward, a little hesitantly. He eyed Neil a trifle nervously. 'You ain't allowed to go driving a wagon train across that land. You were warned by Mister Sherman, yet it seems you went ahead in spite of that. The law says that the wagons, and all goods that they contain, may be confiscated and taken over by the person who had been wronged. In this case, I reckon that's Mister Sherman. In addition, it says that you and the leader of that train can be arrested and charged with–'

'Save your breath, Sheriff,' snapped Neil harshly. 'I ain't ever heard of those laws and neither has anybody else. The Government has given settlers the right of access to the trails that lead to California, and there ain't nobody who can dispute that. If anybody else says different, then I reckon he's just been bribed by Sherman here.'

'Now see here,' began the other harshly. There was a filming of sweat on his flabby features now and Neil could see him glancing towards Sherman as though seeking advice, waiting for the other to back up what he said. 'I'm the elected sheriff in Twin Creeks. If you try to resist arrest, then I'll have to take you in the hard way. Are you coming peaceable, or not?'

Neil shook his head very slowly. 'You ain't got no right to arrest us, Sheriff, and you know it.' His smile was thin and deliberately menacing, and it never touched his eyes.

Sherman said harshly: 'You're only making things worse for yourselves, you know. There are plenty of us to take you in, more men out in the street. Why not see sense and realise when you're licked?' In spite of his words, there was a look of angry defiance in his eyes.

Neil thinned his lips. His fingers were spread wide stiff, like the branches of a tree, hovering only a little way above the twin guns in his belt. He knew that the eyes of every man in the room were on him at that moment, wondering what he intended to do. He knew that the sheriff wasn't too happy about the thought of trying to take him in, even with those men backing him up.

Out of the corner of his eye he saw the bartender edging sideways a little, trying to make the movement as slow and as unobtrusive as he could. He could guess at the reason for the other's actions and he knew that the showdown would come within a minute or two. There would be a shotgun somewhere behind that counter and that once the bartender had his hands on it, he would use it. But first, the other would wait to see what move Sherman intended to make. The blast of a shotgun could make a terrible mess in that confined space and the other would not want to use it unless as a last resort.

Neil grinned at the Sheriff's discomfiture. 'Seems like that man of yours at the back of the bar is tired of livin'. Reckon you ought to warn him that he'll be dead before he can lift that gun out.'

This was more or less what Neil had expected, and yet he knew that Sherman was still hesitating. Maybe the other had figured that if he brought along enough men there would be little chance of the two men making a fight of it. That could be the reason he had come himself, to see that nothing went wrong. Perhaps he was even now beginning to regret that decision. He would know of Neil's reputation and would have realised that if lead did start to fly there, he was right in the middle of it – and such a thought, such personal danger, would not be to his liking. He preferred to send his own hired killers out to do the dirty work for him, to risk their lives, but never his own.

'Thinking about it, Sherman?' put in Neil softly. 'I reckon that you'd better make up your mind pretty quick if you're going to back up your words or stand on one side and let us pass. Because I'm going to count up to five and at the end of that time either shuck your gunbelts or go for your guns. The choice is up to you.'

The rancher glared at him truculently but did not reply right away. Neil saw him run his tongue around his dry lips, then flicker his gaze towards the man standing behind the bar, his hands still in sight on top of the polished bar where Neil could see them. Neil put a hard stare at Sherman, then let his glance slide to the sheriff. The other pulled out a red handkerchief and mopped at his streaming brows. Almost as if it had been a signal, Sherman leapt back, throwing his body to one side, his hands streaking for the guns at his belt.

It was a good draw, a fast draw, but it could not match that of the man who faced him. Even as Sherman threw himself to one side, striking the floor and rolling a little way towards the door, the bullet struck him high in the shoulder, and he uttered a shrill yell of pain, the gun dropping from his nerveless fingers. The other men went for their guns, clawing for them, reacting just as Neil had expected. The initial action had startled these men. For an instant they were motionless. Neil shot now without hesitation. He knew who these men were, knew that they were low-born killers, men like those who had deliberately sent that herd stampeding on to a defenceless wagon train, killing Tom Vance and making a widow of his wife. Two of the men were driven back as the bullets slammed into their chests, their faces relaxing into expressions of frozen amazement, their bodies knocking against those of the men standing behind, sending them off balance, spoiling their aim. A bullet hummed very close to Neil's head, smashed the mirror at the back of the bar into a thousand gleaming fragments.

He caught a glimpse of the bartender leaning to one side, reaching for the shotgun, determined to join in the fray. Then the other suddenly stiffened, seemed to jerk up on to his toes as if reaching instead for the ceiling over his head. His body slumped forward as Jackson spun and drilled him neatly through the head, sending him jerking over the bar, where he lay sprawled with his arms dangling limply in front of him.

Quite clearly Sherman had expected his men to gun down the two men who faced him. Only this was one time when it wasn't going to work. The guns that spoke and roared in that saloon were handled by one of the fastest men in the west, and Jackson was not too far behind when it came to handling his long-barrelled weapons.

The blood began to pound through his ears and along his veins as he thumbed back on the twin hammers, sending bullet after bullet crashing into the men in front of him. They flopped to the floor of the saloon. One man tried to crawl away, still reaching for the gun which had been knocked spinning from his fingers. Without any mercy in his mind at all, Neil shot him down. Now there were only two men left on their feet facing Neil and Jackson. One man stumbled forward, clutching at his stomach as Jackson fired. The other suddenly let go his guns, stepped back a couple of paces and lifted his hands over his head. His face lost colour, became like putty and his eyes took on a startled look of fear.

Neil said easily: 'Just stay right there, nice and easy, mister.'

He saw the man's adam's apple bob up and down as he swallowed thickly, still keeping his hands lifted. On the floor, Sherman pushed himself on to his knees. Blood flowed from the wound in his shoulder, staining the perfect whiteness of his silk shirt. He pressed his fingers tightly over it, but the redness continued to dribble between them and he gritted his teeth with the sudden pain of it, lips pressed tightly together, eyes narrowed to mere slits, as he glared at Neil, then turned his eyes slowly to look at the men who lay beside him.

The fear in his eyes faded slowly, to be replaced by a look of anger, a crafty look that Neil noticed at once. Then there was hatred there, a vitriolic hatred which Neil could not recall having seen in any man's eyes before.

'Reckon you overplayed your hand,' he said softly. 'Seems like you might be needin' a new sheriff around here, too. The last one made the mistake of trying to draw when the odds were stacked against him.' Neil went forward and poked at the short, fat figure on the floor with the toe of his boot. But the sheriff did not move and there was a vacant look in the eyes that stared up at the ceiling, a dead and empty look.

He could see Sherman's thoughts through the rapidly changing expression on the rancher's features. Incredulous disbelief, then the raw and naked fury again as he realised that his men had been killed, shot down by two men who were past craftsmen with a gun. His face was white. Through

150

tight lips, he said harshly and with a savage emphasis: 'I told you when we met the last time that I'd kill you, Roberts. I still mean that.' The words were flat, emotionless things in contrast to the anger written on his chalk-white face. He was still trembling with rage. 'I'll hunt down that wagon train with every man I can lay my hands on, I'll burn it to ashes and destroy every man, woman and child who rides with it. I don't care whether it happens tomorrow or whether I have to follow you all the way to California. I'll finish you, Roberts, and everybody with you.'

'Better get on your feet and move outa here before I lose my patience and plug you,' said Neil with a faint snarl. 'I ain't forgotten what happened when that herd was stampeded against the wagons. I'll never forget that. And I want you to remember this. The next time I see you, whether you've got a gun or not, whether you're wounded or not, I'll shoot you down like the polecat you are.'

Slowly, painfully, the other pushed himself to his feet. He moved over the sprawled bodies on the floor, passed the man who stood with his hands raised in the air, said harshly: 'Stop looking like a goddamned fool, Henson. If he meant to shoot you

151

down he'd have done it before now.'

Reluctantly, keeping his gaze fixed on the gun in Neil's hand, the other lowered his arms, then turned and followed the rancher out of the saloon. The batwing doors swung shut behind them. Neil walked to the door, stared out into the hot, dusty street that ran the full length of the township of Twin Creeks. There was that odd tightness back in his mind now as he dropped the gun back into its pouch. There would be no more warnings on either side. The lines were drawn as far as Sherman and the wagon train were concerned, and the fight was in deadly earnest now. But that was the way it had to be and, inwardly, he knew that it was the way he preferred to have it. Now he knew where he stood, knew that once Jackson got back and told the others what had happened, he would have every man in the train behind him, ready to fight if they had to, because now they would know exactly what they were up against. The chips were down and this was the only way they could ever hope to win.

Sherman walked slowly across the street, the other gunman close on his heels. In front of the glass-panelled door of the sheriff's office directly opposite the saloon they paused, held conversation for several minutes, sometimes pausing to glance back in the direction of the saloon. They were too far away for Neil to be able to pick out any of their conversation, but he guessed that they would soon ride out of town and pick up any other gunslammers that Sherman had on his ranch. Then they would come a-riding after the train. With the humiliation of having been shown up in front of people from the town, and thirsting for revenge, the other would not wait long before making his play.

Sherman untied his horse from the hitching post, mounted, then swung away down the street, dust kicked up from the hooves of his mount obscuring him as he reached the far end and then swung out of town, back along the trail to the east. The gunman who had spoken with him had paused, turned to watch the rancher ride off, then he went inside the sheriff's office and closed the door behind him. For a few moments Neil deliberated that move, then decided that there would be no more trouble from that man for the time being. Evidently Sherman had left him behind in town to keep his eyes open and report back to him everything that happened, particularly when the wagon train moved into town and then continued on its way west. Twin Creeks lay on the very boundary of Sherman's vast cattle empire. West of the town, where the country changed, reaching out as far as the distant mountains, lay the Hollard country. Matt Hollard, a man tarred with the same brush as Sherman. Two sworn enemies, but he had little doubt that when it came to letting a wagon train move across their land, they would temporarily forget their differences and band together against a common enemy.

'You reckon that he'll come riding after us like he said?' asked Jackson, as they went outside on to the wide boardwalk, stood looking about them for a long moment, with the heat of afternoon lying over them.

'I'm sure he will. He'll never rest until he's killed us all. Maybe it would have been better for everyone if I had shot him back there and finished it then.'

'Could be.' The other looked at him from shaded eyes, then his lips twisted into a curling smile. 'But we'll cross that bridge when we come to it, my friend. There is no point in worrying about these trifles.' He clapped a huge hand on Neil's shoulder. 'Now we must see if we can get any supplies. It may be that everyone here is so afraid of Sherman that they won't sell us anything, even though we have the money to pay for it.'

This proved to be true in the first three stores they tried. It was not until they entered the fourth, a smaller place at the far end of the street, that they had any better luck. The middle-aged woman behind the counter eyed them curiously as they went in, glanced at the guns which hung low on their hips, then stared up into Neil's face as if trying to read what she saw there.

'Howdy, Ma'am,' Neil spoke pleasantly. 'We're from the wagon train to the east of town a mile or so back along the trail. We need some supplies, thought you might be able to sell us some.'

She continued to eye him for a moment with a look of frank puzzlement on her face. Then she nodded her head slowly as if in secret understanding. 'There was some shooting down at the saloon a while back,' she said softly. 'I don't suppose either of you two gentlemen had any hand in that. They tell me that crooked sheriff and a dozen or so of the killers who go under the name of deputies around town were gunned down.' She raised her brows a little, the ghost of a smile playing around her lips.

'Reckon you heard right, Ma'am,'

murmured Neil, quietly.

'I thought so. Ain't much I don't hear. They also say that Jesse Sherman was wounded in the fighting and that he's ridden out of town swearing revenge on the men who did it.' Her eyes were shrewd and bright. 'Can't say I've liked that man or what he does around here. Anybody who takes a gun and teaches him a lesson deserves everything this town can give him. Though I doubt if you'll find many people here who'll be willing to help you. They're all too afraid of what Sherman and his men will do to them if he should find out.'

Neil nodded. 'We've already discovered that for ourselves, Ma'am.'

'I thought so.' She paused, then said quietly: 'Well, what is you need?'

'Many thanks, Ma'am,' Neil grinned. He gave her the list of supplies they needed. 'It's good to know that there are some folk at least who aren't afraid of Sherman and what he stands for in these parts.'

'He's an evil man. He'll kill you if he ever gets the chance. Don't underestimate him, whatever you do.'

'We won't,' said Jackson loudly. 'He's ridden out of town but left one of his men in the sheriff's office. Reckon we'd better get back to the train and warn them before it's too late.' He tipped his hat to her, bowing a little from the waist.

Outside, they loaded the supplies on to the waiting horses, untied them from the rail, then swung up into the saddle, heading out of town. Out of the corner of his vision Neil noticed the white face of the gunman staring at them through the window of the sheriff's office, watching them as they rode out of town.

At the wagon train the news spread like wildfire, but strangely there were no dissenting voices when Jackson put the position to them, told them that they had decided to ride west, to finish the drive. But there was a certain hardness in the others now. Neil noticed it, not only with the men – for he had expected it there – but the women too, were hard-faced, as if they had been stung by something so that their pride had been touched. He knew now, with a conviction deep within him, that there could be no turning back for the train now. These people were solidly behind him, would fight every single inch of the way to the California border, facing no matter what lay ahead of them with that singleness of purpose which came from the knowledge that they had right on their side and that whatever happened they would triumph over evil.

'What's the terrain like west of here?' asked Jessup harshly. He chewed on a plug of tobacco, teeth working on it endlessly. He gave Neil a shrewd glance.

'Rugged, I'm afraid. It's Hollard's land but he won't stop Jesse Sherman from riding over it and bringing his killers with him if he knows why Sherman is trailing us.'

'Never figgered he would. Seems the cattle bosses ought to have their tails cut a little. Wonder why there ain't been no Texas Rangers moving into these parts, maybe a straight marshal or two.'

'They'll be along one of these years,' Neil told him. 'Until then, whenever you come up against a crooked sheriff working in cahoots with these killers, there's only one thing you can do. Fight them yourself.'

'Sure. And if they catch you, there'll be a wanted poster out for you, and they'll telegraph your name and description to every sheriff's office in the territory. Even the straight lawmen will be on your trail then and you don't stand much chance proving your innocence to them, do you. Not only the lawmen, but the bounty hunters, too.'

Neil nodded his head slowly, eyes clouded

a little with memory. He left the other and went over to where the sorrel stood waiting. That was how it had been with him several years before. The outlaws had moved into town, bringing their own brand of lawlessness with them, setting up their own sheriff. They had tried to run his father off their small ranch on the outskirts of town, and when Neil had shot four of them down and sent the rest running off with their tails between their legs, he had been arrested and tossed into jail on a charge of murder.

Fortunately, he had still had some friends in town, and one dark and moonless night they had overpowered the two men set to watch his cell and busted him out of jail. He had ridden hard for the ranch, only to find it a smouldering heap of ruin and ashes. His father's body lay in the yard by the well they had dug. The outlaws had ridden back with him out of the way and shot his father down. There were four bullets in his back and he hadn't even had a chance to get a gun to defend himself. It was then that Neil had sworn to hunt down the men who had done that deed, even if it meant searching for them throughout the whole of the territory. But it hadn't taken him as long as that, for they had taken over the town then, set themselves up as the law there. He had gone on a bloody trail of vengeance which ended when ten men lay dead in the dusty streets and there had been only one man left – Jesse Sherman.

Almost of its own volition, his right hand moved down, touched the butt of the gun in its holster, fingers running over the smooth metal, almost caressingly. Killing Sherman had become his own special burden now. It was something which had changed him utterly from the man he had used to be. It had burned most of the humanity out of him, seared through him like a living flame, taking with it any tendency towards mercy and justice. It had made him tough, had forced him to practise with the guns until he had become the fastest and most feared man in the territory. Now he had the reputation of a killer, and yet had never shot a man except in self-defence, and then only men who deserved nothing more.

But he doubted if that reputation would ever leave him. It was something he could never throw off, something indelible like dirt that stuck to a man and changed his entire life, turned a man from a peace-loving citizen into a dedicated killer with a purpose.

How many of the people riding with this

train guessed that, he wondered. There was no doubt in his mind that some of them knew he had a past, perhaps had figured out for themselves that he was wanted by the law, but so long as he made it possible for them to get through to California, then they were prepared to forget that, overlook his past. While he regretted the necessity of bringing Sherman's vengeance down on these people, he knew that he had had no other choice left open to him. Jackson knew that too. He threw a swift glance to where the big man was hefting large bags of flour and beans into one of the wagons. Soon they would be ready to move out. The heat of the day was past and it would be getting cooler. The country that lay directly ahead of them was not easy ground to cover in wagons, and he knew that it would be thirty, maybe forty days before they crossed it and came into the foothills of the tall mountains that formed a vast barrier to their progress.

By then it would be nearing winter, the first snows would be falling up there among the peaks and the narrow passes. There were two passes over the mountains, and they would have to choose one of them. Whichever they chose, it was going to be difficult to cross the mountain barrier, a nightmare of snow and ice, raging blizzards that could bury them.

With an effort he put the thought out of his mind. A lot could happen before then. There were other dangers to be faced, swollen torrents as the rains swelled the rivers, the border gangs who preyed on the wagons that managed to get that far; and, above all, Jesse Sherman, thirsting for revenge, hunting them down with hatred in his heart.

6

Night Ride

Four hours after the long wagon train pulled through Twin Creeks, heading west along the rough trail, a small party of men left the Sherman ranch and rode across country, heading in the same direction, but much further north so that their paths would not cross. Leading the men, Jesse Sherman, ignoring the wound in his shoulder, from which the bullet had been taken that afternoon, his teeth gritted against the pain and his face grey from loss of blood, sat taut and straight in the saddle, gripping the reins with an unnatural tightness with his good hand. The deep-seated anger and the need for revenge drove him on. The doctor who had extracted the lead from his shoulder and patched it up had warned him against leaving his bed for two weeks, had told him that he might not live if he persisted in his wild idea of riding out that night with some of his men, running the risk of opening the wound again, starting the blood flowing into the bandage around his shirt.

Five miles to the west of the ranch they crossed the boundary between his land and that which belonged to Matt Hollard. The uneasy truce which had existed between the two men lasted only so long as neither side made any wrong move along this boundary, but Sherman knew deep within himself that there would be armed men watching every inch of the trail from that point on, and there might be a bullet waiting for him before he could get to the ear of Matt Hollard.

But such was his anger at what had happened back in Twin Creeks that he had thrown all caution to the winds, had deliberately decided to take the risk of being shot from ambush. Before he had ridden out he had debated whether to go alone; knowing that if he went with a bunch of armed men such as this, it might appear that his was a warlike, provocative mission and not a peaceable one as he intended. But he had decided against this. A couple of men might think twice about opening fire on them if there was a large party.

He debated on the wisdom of even approaching Hollard with his proposition, and wondered how the other would take it. But Neil Roberts and that wagon train had moved out of Twin Creeks, was headed west, and if he wanted to stop them, if he was to fulfil the threat he had made, that he would shoot down every man, woman and child in that train, then he would have to cross Hollard's territory to do it, there was no other way open for him. He knew how Hollard hated settlers and nesters just as he did, and there was the chance that the other might listen to reason, might be willing to forget the feud which had existed between them, at least until he had carried out his promise of destruction.

He glanced out of the corner of his eye at the men who rode with him. Grim, determined killers, men he had chosen carefully and well. They would obey every order that he gave, would have no compunction about shooting down unarmed women and children. In fact, he thought with a touch of grim amusement, they might even prefer things that way. It would minimise the risk of any of them being shot down in return.

Two miles further on they crossed a narrow trail which led up into the dark fastnesses of the hills, and he turned his mount deliberately on to it, so that within minutes they were climbing the steep, switchback courses that swung around the side of the hills, looking down on to the rough open plain below. Here they were forced to ride in single file, and as he neared the Hollard ranch he felt his nerves beginning to jump uncontrollably. A lot would depend on Hollard now. He was a strange and unpredictable man at the best of times, a man it was unwise to cross. But he might be inclined to be a little more co-operative now when it came to destroying this wagon train and he knew that Roberts killed some of Hollard's men at some time in the past. It was more than likely that the other would be glad to get rid of him, once and for all.

The wind had built up to powerful gusts here and there was a storm blowing up on the horizon, with brief flashes of lightning running along the dark skyline. Overhead the clouds were gathering, a dark curtain that came sweeping across the sky, blotting out the stars, sending the first heavy drops of rain down on to their heads and into their faces.

Gritting his teeth as a spasm of pain lanced along his arm, Sherman drew his heavy coat tightly around him, knowing the foolishness of trying to hurry along a trail such as this where, in places, only a mule was sufficiently sure-footed to be absolutely safe.

Half a mile on the trail widened, and Trudeau, the ranch foreman, rode up alongside, his face in deep shadow.

'I got the feeling that we're being watched all the way, Mister Sherman,' he said gruffly.

'That's more than likely. They'll have seen us ride in from the ranch over the boundary, but they won't be sure of what we want. That's why they'll hold their fire until they get any orders from Hollard, and I'm figuring that he'll be more than curious to know why we're riding out to see him.'

'You reckon he might agree to your proposal,' Trudeau asked. His voice was quiet and calm, the voice of a man unafraid.

'I don't reckon he's got anything to lose.' Sherman turned quickly. The wind switched from side to side now that they were more in the open, away from the shelter of the lee of the hill, hitting them from one side and then the other like the angry switching of a mare's tail. The rain began to pour on to their heads now, sweeping in sheets down the side of the hill.

'We've got to move if we want to hit the ranch before the storm gets any worse,' Sherman growled. He felt the weakness growing in his body and there was a mist in front of his eyes, a mist which came from the weakness in him, from the blood which had flowed from the gaping hole in his shoulder before the doctor had managed to plug it. The bandage, which had been bound tightly over it, was still warm and sticky where fresh blood had soaked into it, but the anger that drove and spurred him on would not let him rest, would not allow his body to get the sleep it craved so much. There was a lot he had to do before the night was over, and all of it began with Matt Hollard.

They reached the end of the downward trail, came out among the tumbled rocks at the base of the hills. The trail was a grey scar over the darkness of the plain that stretched away in front of them, dimly seen through the driving rain. The heavy drops fell from the brim of his hat, pattered against his face, half-blinding him. The lightning, never ceasing now, speared across the western heavens, bringing the roaring thunder close on its swift heels.

They put the heads of their mounts into it, crouched low in the saddle now, bending over the necks of the horses, hanging grimly to leather as they made their way over the rough terrain.

In spite of their haste, the full fury of the storm swept about them before they reached the Hollard ranch. They rode around the brow of a tall hill which overlooked the ranch house and corral, and were moving slowly when the three dark figures materialised suddenly from the stunted bushes that grew on either side of the trail. Sherman reined his mount instantly, saw Trudeau go for his gun and stopped him with a sharply hissed warning.

'They've got rifles trained on us,' he said harshly. 'Keep your hands away from your guns. I'll deal with this.'

'Now if that ain't real sensible of you,' sneered a deep voice. 'Better ride up here aways, mister, and let me take a look at you – and no tricks, mind, it would be the greatest pleasure for me to put a bullet into you.'

Gigging his mount, Sherman rode forward, said in a soft level voice: 'I'm Jesse Sherman. I've come out here to speak with Hollard.'

'Sherman!' There was a trace of surprise in the other's voice. He kept the barrel of the rifle trained on the other's chest, then came forward a little way, clambering over the smooth, treacherous rocks, wet with rain. He peered up into Sherman's face, then nodded his head slowly, let his breath exhale in a thin whistle through his clenched teeth. 'Now why should you be riding out here to parley with Hollard?' he said, half musingly.

'That's no business of yours,' snapped Sherman. 'Just take us to him.'

'Well, well, now. You seem mighty sure of yourself, Mister Sherman. Maybe you're forgetting whose spread you're on.' The insolence in the other's tone was readily discernible, but Sherman forced himself to ignore it. He was in a very precarious position here and recognised the fact instantly. Even with his men with him, even if he did go for his guns and shot these three men down, there would be more than two dozen others on their backs before they could ride a quarter of a mile, and that was not going to help him with his problem.

'You going to take us to him, or do I have to find him myself and tell him that you tried to stop us from seeing him?' he asked quietly.

For a moment he thought he saw the tight look on the man's face turn nasty and there was a lot of meanness in him as he said: 'All right, mister. Follow me. I must say you were the last man we figured on seeing here.' He turned on his heel, boots rasping on the rock as he led the way down the slope of the hill, across to the corral and the ranch house. There were lights burning in several of the windows, and Sherman could smell smoke in his nostrils as he reined his mount in the courtyard and slid from the saddle, standing weakly by the animal for a long moment, sucking the air down into his gasping lungs as a wave of weakness went through him. Gradually his whole being steadied. He did not want Hollard to see how badly hurt he had been during the fight with Roberts. It might give the other man ideas about taking over the whole of the range in that part of the territory if he figured that he could get him at a disadvantage.

The gunman walked to the door of the ranch and rapped loudly, waited. A moment passed and then the door was flung open and Sherman saw a short, stocky figure outlined against the yellow light from inside. Evidently Hollard was not anticipating trouble otherwise he would never have outlined himself in silhouette like that, inviting a bullet from the darkness.

Hollard hesitated, then walked out into the pouring rain. A flash of lightning picked out his short figure as he made his way across the courtyard until he was standing in front of Sherman. His keen-eyed gaze flickered over the other as he stared at him, the rain streaking his features.

'Slim says that you want to speak to me, Jesse,' he said harshly. 'I reckon it must be something pretty important for you to come riding out here to find me. Better come into the house. We can parley in comfort there.' He turned his head and ran his gaze along the line of men seated in the saddle around him. 'I know you'll understand if I ask your boys to go with mine into the bunkhouse where they'll get themselves a bite to eat and something hot to drink.' A faint smile flickered around the edges of his mouth.

'Sure, sure, Matt.' Sherman gave a quick nod, following the other into the ranch house.

Hollard waved the other towards a chair in the well-lit study at the rear of the ranch. Then he lowered himself into his own chair, let his gaze drop to the bulge of the bandage under Sherman's coat. 'You look as if you've been hurt, Jesse. Not trouble, I hope.'

'Nothing I can't handle, Matt,' acknowledged the other. 'But I'd like your help in this.'

The dark, thick brows lifted a little over the deep-set eyes. 'My help? Now this must be the first time you've ever come asking for that. What sort of trouble is it?'

'Settler trouble and a man called Neil Roberts.' Sherman saw the speculative expression grow in the other man's eyes. Hollard leaned forward over the polished top of the desk in front of him, placed the tips of his blunt spatulate fingers together.

'Roberts. Sure, I seem to recall that name. He made some trouble for me a while ago. Shot some of my best men. I've always wanted to meet him face to face. Where does he fit in with you?' A certain hardness to the other's tone now.

'I want him dead and I want to pull the trigger that sends him into eternity, and I want him to know that it's me who's shot him.'

172

'Did he do that?' Hollard nodded his head in the direction of the bandage around Sherman's shoulder.

The other nodded slowly, lips tightening a shade. 'He killed some of my men and made me look a fool into the bargain, in front of most of the people of Twin Creeks. But there's more to it than that – a lot more. He's leading a wagon train west to California. One of the biggest collection of settlers you've ever seen, and they slipped across my land before I could finish them. I had some of my men stampede a herd of beef at their wagons, but they managed to get into shelter before the steers hit. Now they've passed out of Twin Creeks and are headed over your land.'

Hollard jerked up his head at that. 'Over my territory,' he boomed, rising swiftly to his feet. He stood for a long moment, staring down at the other, then forced himself to relax and sat down again.

'That's right. I know you'd normally go after them yourself. But that's why I'm here. I've got something personal in this. I swore I'd hunt them down and kill them all and fire their wagons around their ears. I want your permission to ride across your land after them and carry out that threat.'

Hollard rubbed a hand down his cheek. There was a thin smile on his lips as he gazed directly at the man in front of him. 'Do you reckon that with that wound you're in any condition to ride out on their trail, Jesse?'

'I'm damned sure I can. I mean to kill Roberts and everybody who's riding with him, particularly a giant of a man called Jackson. No flesh wound is going to stop me.'

'You must hate this man Roberts,' murmured the other. He grinned quickly. 'I never did see eye to eye with you, Jesse, in the past, and that boundary has always been a bone of contention between us. But I guess I could stretch a point here. I have no liking for settlers myself.'

'I figured you might see it that way,' agreed the other. 'In that case, I'll be on my way. That wagon train could make plenty of ground during the night, and the sooner we catch up with 'em the better.'

Hollard gave him a quick, shrewd glance. 'You ain't thinking of riding on after them tonight? Good God, man, you've been hit. There must be a hole in your shoulder the size of my gun barrel and you've obviously lost a lot of blood even riding the trail to get here. They won't get far with this storm blowing up. I'd be surprised if they made it to the river by morning. My guess is that they'll make camp somewhere on this side of the bluff. That river can be real mean if she's full, and right now, with the heavy rains to the north, she's running hard and strong. Roberts is no fool. He won't put those wagons over after dark, not with the rain beating down in a solid sheet, the current running fast in the middle, and the lightning flashing fit to put the fear of all creation in those horses they have pulling the wagons.'

'Do you know Roberts?' inquired the other, getting unsteadily to his feet, trying to hold himself tautly upright, not to show Hollard just how badly hurt he was. There seemed no point in showing just how much in this man's power he really was. The friendship which the other had extended did not go very far below the surface. Deep down inside, Hollard hated him just as much as he disliked the other man.

Hollard frowned suddenly. 'I've heard a lot about him in the past three, maybe four years. Is there anything more to know?'

'I reckon that I know him better than any other man alive, maybe even better than he knows himself. He'll put that wagon train across the river even at the height of this storm and in total darkness, too, because he knows I'll be riding out after him, and he knows that I can have more men with me than he can stand up against unless he can choose his own defensive ground. That's why he won't really rest until he's over that river and there's one natural barrier between us.'

'Suit yourself,' growled the other harshly. 'It's your funeral. If you want to risk your life going after him right now, when I don't reckon you need to, that's up to you. Do you need any more men to go with you?' He looked directly at the other as he spoke, eyes lidded, speculative.

Sherman hesitated, then shook his head quickly. 'I figure we can handle them,' he said decisively. 'He shot down some of my boys on the eastern edge of my spread and I've a few men with me who want a chance to get him in their sights.'

A fresh gust of wind from up the mountain rocked the branches of the trees that grew on the edge of the spread around the ranch house as Sherman remounted and waited for the rest of his men to put in an appearance. They came straggling from the direction of the long, low bunkhouse to find him in an evil humour, sitting tight in the saddle, lips twisted a little in a dark scowl. The light from the doorway of the ranch showed Hollard standing there, a thin black cheroot between his lips, looking out at them.

'Get mounted!' he called sharply. 'We're riding on after that wagon train.'

A flurry of wind and rain caught his words and whipped them away into the darkness. His sodden clothing clung to his body as he leaned forward in the saddle. Behind him the men climbed grumbling into the saddle, urged their mounts forward, raking spurs over the horses' flanks. They pushed on along the narrow, winding trail that led over the low hill, and as he rode Jesse Sherman peered straight ahead of him, pushing his sight into the rain-soaked darkness, trying to pick out the man he intended to hunt down and kill. For a moment, with the rest of the men around him in a tight bunch, he reached down with his left hand and touched the hard, cold metal of the Colt, fingering it almost caressingly, lips tightened into a thin, hard line across the middle of his features. The rain beat down against the wide-brimmed hat and ran into his eyes, and he brushed it away with an irritated impatient gesture.

As they reached the top of the hill the wind built up into powerful gusts which tore at them from all sides. More than ten miles ahead of them lay the river, and Sherman felt the impatience building up in him as he realised just how much of a lead the train had over him because of that forced stopover at Hollard's ranch. He felt certain that Roberts might decide to put the team into the water that night, refusing to let them make camp until they were all on the far side. Hollard's opinion that the train would hole up for the night near the bluff he did not believe for a single instant.

He drove the men with him, at a savage, cruel pace, punishing the mounts, forcing them to the limit. He knew that the men with him were grumbling at his insistence on continuing to ride in that weather, but he ignored them. They would obey every order he gave, no matter how foolish or unnecessary they considered it to be, because they had no other choice.

At the back of his mind, however, there was a nagging little thought which would not give him peace. Had he made a mistake in asking Hollard's permission to ride out over his territory? Would it not have been in his own interests to have simply cut across country after the train in the hope that they could do so without being spotted by any of Hollard's men? Now Matt Hollard knew that he was headed west after Roberts and the wagon train, knew that he had most of his best men with him, that his own ranch and spread would be virtually unguarded. There was nothing to prevent the other from mustering as many of his men as he could and riding out east, burning and destroying, as he had sworn to do so many times in the past.

It was only with a tremendous effort that he succeeded in putting the thought out of his mind and concentrating on the task in hand, riding down that wagon train and destroying it utterly.

An hour passed. Then another, and still the rain poured out of the dark and overcast sky. The horses covered the distance quickly, but not swiftly enough for Jesse Sherman, who kept urging his men on at a breakneck pace, over rough country that would have tried the endurance of any mount in broad daylight; and now, at night, in that terrible weather, it was a hundred times worse for the tired animals and rain-soaked men. At times

Sherman halted his group, held up his hand for silence and listened, trying to pick out the rumble of wheels on the wet earth, a sound which would tell him whether they were close to the wagon train. But he heard nothing, and the knowledge came to him that they had already reached the river, were possibly crossing it at that moment.

A night crossing – rain and wind and total darkness, with all of its hidden thousand dangers and fears. There was no moonlight to show the river in its full flood, the white, sweeping foam where it plunged over the needle-sharp rocks of the river bed, the logs which were being borne down by the current from further upstream.

Riding to the ribbed bank of the river where the plunging, sweeping water had eaten into the soil, Neil stared about him, taking in everything. Vivid flashes of lightning lit the scene, showed him the boiling, bubbling water in front of him, dull, cold brilliance against the dark background of rocks.

'You reckon it would be wise to try to cross in this storm?' Jackson came riding up, turned his head a little to peer directly at the man who sat tall and straight in the saddle at his side. 'It could be dangerous.'

'We've got to reach the other side before Sherman gets here with his band of killers,' gritted Neil harshly. 'We've no choice.'

'You think he'll come tonight?'

'He'll come, make no mistake about that. He'll be riding out on our trail right now, with as many gunhawks as he could collect. They won't stop until they've caught up with us. That's why I feel we have to put the river between them and us as soon as possible, certainly before morning.'

'I suppose you know best.' Jackson threw a swift, apprehensive glance in the direction of the raging torrent in front of them, then wheeled his mount and galloped back to the wagon train, waiting a hundred yards away. A flash of lightning showed them clearly to Neil as he glanced behind him, the wagons outlined brilliantly against the glare, the canvas tops gleaming white, the horses in the traces, heads drooping, the rain steaming off their flanks.

It would be men's work getting those wagons safely over the swollen river. The danger was there, hanging over them all. And behind them, drawing closer with every passing second, came Sherman and his gunslingers, thirsting for revenge.

Rain dripped in an endless curtain from the

low clouds as the first of the wagons moved slowly, hesitantly, down the river bank and into the swirling water. It was characteristic of Jackson that he sat on the tongue of that wagon and drove it into the sweeping current himself. Neil would never have thought it could have been otherwise. Whatever else Clem Jackson lacked it was certainly not courage and he would never ask any man to do what he was afraid to do himself.

Slowly at first, then faster as though hurried along by the brief flashes of lightning and the booming roll of thunder as it roared over the hills, the wagon moved into the middle of the raging torrent. The horses plunged and reared at the tremendous weight of water, thrust down by the current, caught them on the side, threatening to hurl them sideways, to bring the top-heavy canvas of the wagon toppling down.

Neil sat tightly in the saddle, watched through narrowed eyes as the wagon moved deeper into the river. For a moment he saw the wagon sway dangerously to one side as a wheel struck a hidden rock under the water. The rushing water attacked it hungrily, struck with a titanic force; then, miraculously, the wagon righted itself, continued forward until it dragged itself, dripping, up the other bank.

One by one the other wagons in the train began the crossing. Neil watched tensely. At any moment danger could strike and a wagon, possibly more, could go tumbling into that foaming water and be washed away before they could get a lariat around it and bring it back upright. For a while everything went well. Most of the wagons had crossed, were safely on the other side. There were only four left to move over, four and Neil himself.

A half-hour. Twenty minutes. Then the last two wagons were moving slowly and unsteadily across. Neil waited for a moment, then put his horse into the water. It moved strongly forward, sure-footed, keeping its balance with ease. The tension grew in Neil's mind. It only needed one mistake, one piece of ill fortune and–

It happened suddenly and without warning and although he had half-expected trouble, it came with the shock of the unexpected. He heard the shouts of the men and women on the wagons, could just glimpse their white and frightened faces in the flashing lightning that seared across a heaven gone berserk. Then the last wagon suddenly tipped over to one side. The horses struggled in the traces, tried to keep their balance against the dragging weight of the overturning wagon. The shrill scream of the woman inside rose to Neil's ears.

'Hold those horses steady!' he yelled, shouting at the top of his voice, but the warning was drowned out by the peal of thunder which broke almost directly overhead, and the warning came too late, anyway, to save those in the wagon. Crashing into the water, it turned over and over, the white canvas, sodden with the water, curling and flapping about it as the current caught it and carried it unresisting downstream. The horses suddenly broke free of the leather, struggled upright, neighing in fright, swam for the further bank.

Turning his own mount, Neil plunged down towards the overturned wagon, his lariat whirling in his right hand. He caught a brief glimpse of the white arm upraised from the smashed Conestoga, tried to make a cast, but the wind caught it, deflected his throw and the noose fell short. Then there was nothing he could do. Those in the wagon were lost. Wearily he wound the riata, coiled it back into place. There was a deep weariness in him as he made his way to the bank.

Jackson came stumping back, rain puddling about his feet. He stared up at Neil, blinking the water from his eyes, wiping it swiftly from his face with the back of his hand.

'There was nothing I could do for them,' said Neil dully.

'I understand.' Jackson nodded. There was a curious expression on his face and Neil noticed the way he suddenly averted his gaze, as though afraid to meet Neil's directly.

Neil kept them on the move, knowing that the best thing now was for the people in the train to work and not to think of what had happened. Soon, perhaps in the morning, they would have time in which to realise that some of their friends had died during the night, their bodies carried away by the sweeping current.

Three hours later he called a halt. They were almost five miles from the river on a wide stretch of ground, raised a little from the surrounding terrain, to form a miniature plateau. Overhead the storm clouds rolled from horizon to horizon and there seemed to be no place where they could get dry. It was dangerous to light a fire, and they settled down, shivering, waiting for the grey light of dawn to bring an end to their discomfort.

Five miles to the east Jesse Sherman reined his mount, peering through the teeming rain, looking down at the river where it stormed between its banks in the darkness. Sucking in his lips, swaying in the saddle from weariness and weakness, he turned and gazed at the men who had ridden with him. Tired men who had ridden far and hard. But they had to go on. The river faced them and there was a dull ache in his body which refused to leave him now, something which had always been there since they had set out on this ride and which had grown over the miles and the hours.

'There's one of the wagons down by the bend a couple of hundred yards down-stream,' said one of the men. 'They've crossed the river and could be miles away by now.'

'That wagon back there? What happened?'

The other shrugged. 'Must have hit a rock in midstream. Nobody still alive and I doubt if anybody got out of it. They never stood a chance. Roberts seems determined to push ahead, even if it mean killing some of 'em on the way.'

'He knows we're around, close on his heels,' murmured the other grimly. He pulled his cloak more tightly about him as gusts of wind pulled at his clothing.

'Do we cross now?' asked another man

thinly. 'Since we're in this as deep as you are, I reckon we ought to know just why we're after this wagon train. I know you're intent on killin' Roberts. That's understandable. But what about the train?'

Sherman looked him over deliberately. He said: 'You seem to be acting damned big at the moment. Are you workin' for me, or aren't you?? Remember, I can turn you over to the law and then you're finished.'

'I'm working for you,' affirmed the other, 'but I'd like to know why we're going out to shoot up unarmed women and kids. I've a hankering for bigger game than that.' He spoke boastfully, fingering the gun in his belt, ignoring the rain that slashed at them. He stared challengingly at Sherman. 'I'd have preferred to have a gamer chance with some of Hollard's men.'

'You may get that chance before long,' Sherman promised. 'But right now we have another job to do. Go after that wagon train and finish it off. I don't want a single person left alive when we're done.'

The man nodded, relaxed a little. 'You must hate Roberts to do something like this.'

Sherman forced a tight grin. That was the second time that night someone had said that to him. Yes, he thought savagely, with a tightening of the muscles of his arms, he hated Roberts, meant to see him dead before morning. With a sharp yell, he urged the men into the river, putting his own mount into the storming current. The river was so swollen in the middle that they were forced to swim their horses, and the current carried them almost fifty yards downstream before they climbed the further bank.

The storm increased as they hit the trail and started west, their horses plunging and rearing in spite of all they could do to calm them. Such terrible pounding storms had plagued this stretch of country for centuries, had been one of the natural scourges of the west. Storms that blew up swiftly, clouds running before the wind, bringing solid sheets of rain, great splashing streaks of lightning bolts and such savage roaring thunder that they were one experience which startled newcomers to these parts and were never forgotten by those who had the misfortune to ride through them.

Sherman forced himself to hold on tightly to the reins, leaning forward over his mount's neck. The drenching rain never ceased to pound at them. The lightning showed them the trail, the streaking bolts searing across the sky in an almost continual succession.

He pushed his sight ahead of him as far as he could whenever the vivid flashes lit up the terrain around them, a wild and rugged landscape of tumbled rocks and tall canyon walls, etched and fluted by long ages of wind and rain, where erosion had bitten deeply into the sandstone. Gusts of wind caught at them and threatened to hurl horse and rider from the trail, into the brush that rose up on either side. But by the light of the flashing lightning it was possible to see the deep ruts where the wheels of the heavy wagons had bitten deeply into the soft, muddy earth. Already they were filling rapidly with water. He kicked spurs along the flanks of his mount, galloped him into the darkness.

Half an hour later they followed the trail more slowly and warily. Sherman had the unshakeable feeling that the wagon train lay only a short distance ahead and he was not anxious to stumble upon it without warning. That could be asking for trouble if they had guards posted, although in this weather and after so long a ride, he doubted if the guards would be quite as watchful as Roberts would have wished. Still, there was no point in taking any unnecessary risks. Roberts himself and that great bearded giant might be on watch and they were a different proposition. They would never sleep while there was any danger to the train. He felt the tightness in his body once more, felt for the butt of the gun at his hip, and cursed the wound in his shoulder which made it almost impossible for him to use his right arm now. A half-cripple might stand little chance against a man such as Roberts, and yet he was determined that it should be his gun that killed the other and that Roberts should know he had pulled the trigger.

He turned things over in his mind as he rode, forming plans and then rejecting them almost instantly. He would have to rely on one of his men disarming Roberts. Then he would step in and take over. Every one of his men had explicit orders on that particular point. He wanted to kill Roberts. They had only to wound or disarm him. He would do the rest. His lips curled at the thought, at the sweetness of revenge.

Then they had topped a low rise and the vivid flash of lightning which lit up the whole heavens showed them the scene below. Less than half a mile from where they stood lay the wagon train. There was no mistaking the white canvas that flapped sluggishly in the wind. A slight shiver went through him as he narrowed his eyes against the glare. Then the lightning died and the darkness was deeper and more intense than before. He could see nothing, his eyes still dazzled.

'There they are,' said Trudeau. 'Right where I would have figured they'd be. He's no fool, that *hombre*. He know the best place in the territory to put a wagon train where it's going to be most difficult to take 'em by surprise.'

'He's no fool,' grated Sherman, 'but in spite of that, he's soon going to be dead and I mean to be the one to kill him. Don't you forget that – any of you.'

'You figuring on riding in there right now, running 'em down before they know we're here?'

'Now I know you're a goddamn fool,' snapped the other. 'They'll have guards on look out. If you want to get yourself shot, just try riding in like that.'

'Then what do we do? Sit it out here for the rest of the night?'

'We go down on foot. Get rid of the guards first. Once they're out of the way the rest ought to be simple. Then we'll be able to take the train by surprise. That way, even Roberts will be unable to stop us.'

He lowered himself unsteadily from the saddle, stood for a long moment, ashen-faced, steadying himself against the heaving flanks of the horse, sheltered a little from the wind and rain there. The pain in his shoulder lanced through his body now and his legs seemed to be losing their starch, unable to go on bearing his weight. Somehow, he forced himself to move forward, one leg in front of the other, walking stiffly, slowly, keeping his blurred vision focused on the wagon train in the distance, as if he needed something to maintain his iron will and determination to keep his tired, weary body moving.

7

Vengeance in Gunsmoke

Neil twisted in his blankets. Lying under one of the wagons, seeking some shelter from the teeming rain, some tiny sound penetrated into that part of his brain which never slept. It was only the faintest whisper of sound but it was sufficient to wake him, his right hand moving out towards the Colt, which lay in its holster within easy reach at the same moment that he eased himself up on to one elbow, wide awake, eyes peering into the darkness about him. He moved his legs a little then eased himself upright, standing by the side of the wagon, the Colts in his hands, every nerve stretched taut, every sense alert, seeking the source of the trouble, the danger. There was the soft clop of hooves in the distance as men rode close, then halted their mounts.

He wondered what had happened to the two men he had placed on guard. Probably asleep by now, wearied by that long ride, by the danger of crossing the swollen river, thinking there could be no danger for what man would ride after them in that teeming rain, with the heavens open above them. They had clearly overlooked the driving hatred which could exist in the soul of a man such as Jesse Sherman, a man who would ride through hell itself to get his revenge.

At the edge of camp he caught glimpse of Calder, one of the men on watch. He was seated on a large boulder, his Winchester between his knees, trying to build himself a smoke in the rain. A second later a coiled rope fell over his shoulders, pinning his arms to his sides, hauling him out of sight.

Neil's two shots, aimed high into the air,

woke the wagon train. Then there was the roar of gunfire from all sides and he threw himself down behind the wagon with a savage curse on his lips. He ought never to have allowed those two men to have taken watch, he ought to have known that they would be half asleep, would not keep a good look out with the rain pouring down on them, with the belief that the nearest danger was many miles away, and would not catch up with them before morning.

He heard the bull-like voice of Clem Jackson yelling a harsh warning, saw him go charging forward between two of the wagons, his long-barrelled Winchester clutched in his huge hands, bringing it to bear on two gun-hawks who came leaping among the rocks, firing as they ran forward. Bullets hummed about Neil as he picked himself up and flung himself forward. More pecked at the wet ground near his feet, or cut through the flapping canvas close to his head.

A dark figure stumbled forward from the direction of the rocks. Swiftly he brought the Colts to bear, squeezed the trigger, saw the other fall forward, the guns in his hands hammering savagely as he pressed down on the triggers with the last ounce of strength in his body. The brief orange flares from the guns showed in the teeming darkness. Then more gunfire had broken out to the rear of the wagons, and he knew they were surrounded.

Jesse Sherman's harsh voice yelled from the darkness; 'You're finished, Roberts. Better throw down your guns and come out here with your hands lifted. The same goes for everybody else. If you don't, then I'll have to kill everybody in the wagon train. You wouldn't want me to do that, would you?'

'You'll do it whether we throw down our guns or not,' yelled Jackson harshly before Neil could answer. A rifle shot bucketed though the silence as the other fired in the direction of the voice.

Now the men in the wagons were firing and some of the women had guns too, were shooting at the shadows of the gunmen hidden among the rocks in the darkness, aiming for the orange flashes which gave away the positions of the gunhawks. Sherman and his men were well hidden, had evidently crept up on the train in the darkness, hoping to take them completely by surprise, would have done so had Neil not picked out the faint sound of horses in the near distance.

Everyone was shooting now, firing and

loading – firing and loading. Six-guns answered from the boulders. Near the edge of the train Neil ran forward, crouched over until he came to where Jackson lay on his stomach, pumping shots slowly and methodically into the rocks.

'Follow me!' he said harshly. 'We've got to take them out there, before they shoot down everyone in the train.'

Jackson nodded, understood in an instant, crawled forward after him. The lightning was retreating to the eastern horizon as the storm passed over. The rain was not so heavy now and there was a faint pencil of grey light in the east where the dawn was beginning to break. The air was still cold and beneath their bodies the ground ran with water.

Neil sucked in a long, heavy gust of wind, let it come out through his nostrils in slow pinches. Someone moved directly ahead of him and a moment later he made out the shapes of three men, crouched down behind the rocks. He touched Jackson's sleeve, nodded in their direction.

Some sixth sense must have warned one of the men of the danger for he whirled swiftly, loosing off a single shot that scorched past Neil's cheek, before Jackson blasted with his

196

rifle. One man pitched backward with his arms outflung, hung against the rock at his back for a long moment, before sliding on to the rocky floor at the foot of the boulders. The other two tried to bring their guns to bear, died as Neil squeezed the triggers of his six-guns, felt them buck against his wrists. More ricochets whined off the rocks, jagged fragments of metal that hummed through the night.

There was confused shouting in the distance as more of the gunhawks came under fire from the wagons. Evidently the gunslingers had not expected this savage return fire and were finding things a little too hot for them. Out of the corner of his eye Neil saw two men darting back over the uneven ground to where their horses were evidently waiting. Neither of the men was Sherman. He began to wonder about the other. Sherman had been hit badly in the shoulder during that fight in the saloon back in Twin Creeks, and he must have lost a lot of blood. That, coupled with the hard riding they had evidently put in during the night, meant that he would be as weak as a kitten, would still be holed up somewhere among the rocks waiting a chance to shoot him down from ambush.

He crept forward to the end of the narrow chasm in the rocks, with Jackson following close on his heels, reloading the Winchester. The shouting went on. There was the sound of feet scraping among the rocks less than ten yards away to their right. A burst of gunfire, then a regular fusillade of shots pouring into the wagons. The gunfire rose to a smothering racket that seemed to come from every direction, with the echoes bouncing back from the rearing, rocky walls that lay about them. Drawing his breath, Neil fired into the rocks, saw a dark shadow lurch to one side clutching at a smashed wrist, the gun clattering to the rocks at the man's feet. He clawed for the other Colt with his good hand, but before he could draw it clear of leather another shot took him in the chest and he went down, to stay down.

Gradually the shooting was dying down. The gunmen with Sherman had no stomach for this kind of fighting, with the odds stacked a little too much against them. When it came to shooting down women and children, then they thought nothing of it, but several of their number had been killed, and even Sherman must have realised that they were in a tight spot. More slugs beat through the air as the gunhawks made one last attempt to locate Jackson and Neil, to drill them before they could cause any more trouble. But they might just as well have tried to hit a pair of shadows.

For several minutes shots sounded in ragged, uneven rhythm from the rocks. A man seated on the lip of one of the wagons suddenly gurgled and swayed to one side. Neil saw the woman behind him lean out of the canvas, grab him by the shoulders and haul him back into the wagon. Now the answering fire from the rocks had dwindled until there were only a handful of isolated shots that tore through the canvas or hammered off the wooden upright and shafts. Crouched down among the rocks, eyes straining to pick out any of the gunhawks, Neil heard the thunder of hooves in the distance, heard the horses move away over the crest of the small plateau and then towards the tall hills in the distance.

He drew in a deep breath and lowered the guns, then thrust them back into the holsters. Beside him, Jackson got to his feet, stood with his legs braced against the earth, staring out after the retreating horses. His shoulders moved, swaying a little, as his eyes continued to search through the drizzling rain. Then he gave a quick nod of satisfaction.

'I reckon they had enough,' he said dully. 'I don't figure they'll come this way again in a hurry.'

'I'll feel safer if I know what happened to Sherman. Take a look and see if he's dead. If he is, he'll be lying somewhere in the rocks. I'll go down to the train and check on the casualties there.'

Slowly he moved back into the ring of wagons. There was movement there now. Men who had been wounded by the flying bullets that had torn through thin, flimsy canvas, torn into flesh and bone and sinews. Women were busy tearing up long strips of cloth with which to bind up the wounds that bubbled red. Neil's keen gaze took in everything in a single, wide sweep. Several men had been wounded, but no one killed. They had beaten off Sherman and his gunmen, had whipped them in the rain-drenched darkness. He felt a wave of elation pass through him, a feeling that vanished instantly and utterly as a familiar voice behind him, from near one of the wagons, said:

'Don't make a move for your guns, Roberts. I've got the drop on you and I only need the slightest excuse to kill you.'

Very slowly, without turning, Neil moved

his hands away from the guns at his waist. He knew that there was one gun trained on him at that moment, that he could not possibly draw and fire before the other man, weak and wounded as he may have been, fired and the slug found his heart. But for a moment the idea lived in his mind, then was forgotten.

'Better not tell any of your men to do anything foolish. This gun is trained on your heart and I can kill you long before they shoot me. That goes for the big *hombre* up there.'

Neil lifted his head a little, saw Jackson standing a few yards away, with the Winchester cradled in his arms.

'Drop it, Clem,' he said sharply. 'He means what he says.'

Slowly, reluctantly, the other let go of the rifle so that it fell clattering to the dirt at his feet. His eyes glared at the man standing behind Neil.

'That's being sensible.' There was a harsh laugh from the other. 'All right, Roberts, turn round now but very slowly and easy. I'm going to shoot you down like I swore I would, but I want you to be facing me when I pull this trigger.'

Neil ran his tongue over his dry lips as he

turned very slowly to face the other. Sherman stood a few yards away in front of one of the wagons, a Colt in his left hand, the barrel trained on his heart, the other's hand rock steady in spite of the greyness of his features and the limp right arm hanging by his side.

'And what do you figure is going to happen to you even if you do shoot me, Sherman?' he asked, keeping his voice steady and even. 'You'll be dead the next minute, I suppose you know that. Your men have left you, run out on you. By now they'll be miles away and they won't be coming back to help you.'

Sherman thinned his lips, drew them back over his teeth. 'They've served their purpose now,' he said harshly. He swayed a little, then snapped up the barrel of the Colt sharply as Neil made a slight movement forward. 'I've been waiting for this moment for a long time. I want you to crawl and cringe this time as I had to do all those years ago.'

There was no answer from Neil. He waited, turned his gaze for a moment over the faces of the men and women standing around the wagons. There were no words from any of them. Not that he had expected any. No movement. Sherman drew a rasping breath in through his nostrils and stood erect with an effort. There was a growing red stain on the front of his shirt, a tell-tale bulge where the thick bandage had been wound tightly around his shoulder in an attempt to staunch the flow of blood.

'I'm going to kill you, Roberts.' It was simply said, and there was the promise of death in the other's eyes as he took a single step forward, his finger bar-straight on the trigger of the gun in his hand, knuckles growing white with the pressure he was exerting. Neil braced himself for the impact of the bullet. His eyes locked with those of the man who intended to kill him, waiting, watching, probing for the sign which would tell him that death was on its way. Silence crowded down on the wagon train.

Then there came the sharp, searing blast of a gun. Involuntarily, Neil winced, stiffened, then stared as Sherman fell forward, the gun slipped from his fingers. Slowly, as though every muscle in his body was reluctant to fight against the need to hold him upright, he crashed to the wet ground.

Neil touched his lips with a dry tongue, went forward and stared down at the body of the man who lay in front of him, stretched out at his feet. Then he lifted his head and stared at the wagon directly behind where Sherman had been standing, saw the canvas part and someone step forward with a smoking rifle in her hands.

His eyes held in bewilderment on her as she stood framed in the opening. Then he recognised her, knew why she had killed Jesse Sherman, why she had taken that rifle which had belonged to her husband and shot him in the back.

Very slowly, like a woman in a dream, Claire Vance lowered the hand which held the rifle and stood looking about her in stunned surprise. Out of the corner of his eye Neil saw two of the women move towards her, take the gun from her and lead her gently back inside the wagon.

Jackson came forward, tall and massive, looked down at the dead man with a hard expression on his pitiless features. Then he gave a slow, ponderous nod of his head. 'A strange kind of justice, I suppose,' he said slowly, choosing his words with care. 'But I for one can understand why she killed him.'

Neil gave an answering nod. 'She saved my life,' he said softly.

'Somehow, I doubt if that was the reason she did it. She knew he was the man who was directly responsible for setting that herd on us when her husband was trampled to death by those stampeding steers. Perhaps she'll find some rest now, poor soul.'

The next morning they broke camp, moved out along the trail to the west. The storm had passed and the sunrise was one in which all of the colours seemed to have been washed clean by the rain, flaming reds and oranges which lit up the whole of the eastern horizon. In front of them, almost seventy miles away, the tall peaks of the mountains lifted clear to the blue heaven, their peaks glistening in the brilliant sunlight which touched them with a touch of red, while still leaving the bases in shadow.

Once they reached those mountains, Neil reflected, they would have to move up through one of the two passes open to them. He felt the tiny wave of apprehension flowing in him again. It would take them the best part of thirty-five days to cover that distance because, from his knowledge of the territory, the going became rougher the closer they got to that high range and their progress would be slowed to a crawl during the last ten days or so. By that time the winter would be on them and the first snows would be falling up there among the passes.

If they were caught in one of the early winter blizzards, they might find themselves trapped, and even if they did manage to get safely over to the other side of those mountains, which formed a natural barrier along the trail, they would have the marauding border gangs to contend with, professional killers who owed allegiance to no one and preyed on any wagon trains which managed to get through as far as that.

They had only one slim chance of beating the winter snows among those high passes. He would have to drive the train hard, harder than they had been driven so far, and once again, as far as the others were concerned, the danger was one they would not readily appreciate. A man could see danger when it consisted of bullets drumming at him from the darkness around a ring of wagons, or when it lay in the swirling foam of a swollen river, built high by the heavy rains to the north. But talk of snow which might be there more than seventy miles away and it did not seem to present any real danger.

Fifteen days on the trail. Long days with short nights. Neil had set the hard pace, anxious to cross the plain as quickly as possible, driving man and beast to the utmost limit. They camped wherever they happened to be at midnight, woke with the first grey light of an early dawn, ate quickly, hitched up the teams and moved on again, keeping to the trail that led due west.

Seated by the blazing fire, on the night of the fifteenth day after their brush with Jesse Sherman, Clem Jackson said quietly: 'Some of the men have been grumbling about the way you're driving 'em, Neil. They figure that there ain't so much hurry that we have to drive more'n fifteen hours every day. By the time we reach the mountains, none of the wagons will be in any fit condition to make it over them. We'll have to carry out extensive repairs, and that will take time. You'll lose more time with that than you'll gain pushing them as you are doing at the moment.'

'Do you think I haven't considered that?' Neil spoke with an unaccustomed sharpness, then forced himself to relax. 'Sorry, but I guess I am a little jumpy.'

'You afraid of what we might find when we hit those mountains?' The other raised thick, bushy eyebrows, regarded Neil quizzically.

'Guess so. I made an agreement to get you

folk through to California. We lost some on the way here, mostly my own fault. I had no right letting any of my personal feuds interfere with this, specially as far as Sherman was concerned. That's been the main cause of all our trouble so far.'

'You ain't got nothing to reproach yourself for on that account,' declared the other. 'We all realised that Sherman or Hollard would have killed us all if they had the chance. They're as much against settlers as they were against you.'

'If we run into bad conditions up there in the mountain passes, we may have to spend the whole of the winter this side of 'em. Reckon we don't have enough supplies for that, so the only chance we have is to keep on going. That's why I'm pushing everybody as hard as they can go. I'd like you to try to make them see that. I don't like keeping up this cruel, punishing pace any more than they do. But it won't be long before the first winter storms start up there.'

'Anybody tried to cross during the winter months?' The other teased a strip of beef with the tip of his long-bladed knife, then pushed it into his mouth and chewed on it reflectively.

'Some,' Neil admitted. 'They didn't get far

if we can believe the reports that came back. The blizzards struck while they were crossing, caught them unawares, blocked the pass completely. None of 'em managed to get through to the plains on the far side.'

'And you reckon there's a good chance of that happening to us?'

'I reckon so. We may be lucky. The storms may be late in starting this year.'

A pause, then: 'But you don't think they will be? Is that it?'

'Judgin' from the rivers, they're pretty full at the source up there in the mountains. That's always a bad sign. Could mean an early winter.'

There was no more talk at the fire that night. With the long days on the trail, men snatched at sleep whenever they could. An hour lost in talk meant a tired man the next day, a man whose reflexes were just that shade slower than they ought to have been and that could spell danger.

Wrapped in his blankets, feeling the wind that blew off the mountains blowing cold against his body, Neil Roberts tried to figure out in his mind the best thing to do for the safety of the train. Had it not been for Jesse Sherman, they might have picked up more supplies back in Twin Creeks, might have enough to wait out the worst months of the winter, at least, before attempting the dangerous crossing of those tall, snow-covered peaks. As it was, they had very little left. Perhaps just sufficient to carry them through to the end of the trail, but little besides. There could be no question of waiting it out. Half of them would starve before the weather changed for the better and allowed them to go on with their journey, and he doubted if they could shoot enough to keep themselves alive.

No, they had to cross the peaks and once he had made that decision there was the question of which pass to choose. The pass which slashed through the upper reaches of the mountains directly ahead of them would be the very devil in the midst of winter, was certainly the shortest route, but the more dangerous. The other was easier to negotiate, but it meant swinging to the south, more than two extra days on the drive. He fell asleep with the thoughts still spilling through his mind.

Ten days later they left the trail, struck out across more rugged country leading to the south. Neil Roberts had made his decision. He told Jackson and Jessup of it as they moved off through the rough terrain, the wagons bouncing and jolting over the stony ground.

'We daren't risk taking the wagons over Snake Pass,' he said quietly, eyeing the big man who sat the tongue of the wagon beside him, his own sorrel moving alongside. 'A couple of thrown wheels up there and we would be bogged down for weeks before we could make repairs. At least this way we stand a better chance of getting through without mishap. The South Pass is lower, if there is snow it ought to be less severe than to the north.'

'We're in your hands as far as that is concerned,' muttered the other harshly. He stared ahead, his jaw jutted forward. They had covered several hundred miles now, and somewhere on the other side of that tall range of mountains lay California, the Promised Land, the country where the climate was always mellow and sunny, where the rich red gold had been found. It was enough to fire the imagination of any man, and watching him out of the corner of his eye, Neil could almost read the other's thoughts, knew that most of the men and women in the train were thinking along the same way now that they were approaching the end of their long journey across a continent.

In a way, he felt the empty coldness in his own mind. For him, it seemed, there would always be the wandering, the leagues of rolling grass or the white alkali of the stretching, flat deserts, a man hunted by the law, framed by a crooked sheriff, and always on the run.

'Do you reckon that the folk here can take that journey over the mountains?' he asked abruptly. 'So far, the going has been easy compared with what we'll find up there.'

'They'll take it,' said the other emphatically. 'They knew what they were letting themselves in for before they started out on this trip. You ain't reckoning on any of 'em wanting to turn back now, are you?'

'I was wondering about folk like Claire Vance. There wouldn't seem to be much left for her in California.'

The big man caught Neil's look, shrugged. 'You may be right. Whenever you set out on something like this, there's always somebody who has to get hurt. I suppose she was one of the unlucky ones.'

'How is she taking it now – after what happened with Sherman, I mean?'

Jackson pursed his thick lips. 'I got Virginia Millais taking care of her. She seems to have got over it pretty well considering the shock she must have had. You worried about her, Neil?'

'In a way. She's been through a lot and I feel, well, sorta responsible for her. After all, she did save my life by shooting Sherman. If she hadn't done that he would have shot me down in cold blood.'

'She's back in the fourth wagon if you'd care to take a look-see for yourself. Maybe you'd be able to get her to snap out of it a little.'

He gave Neil a queer look which the other pointedly ignored. Then Neil had swung his legs over the side of the shafts and dropped lightly to the ground, waiting while the other wagons rolled past him, kicking up the grey dust as they rumbled by. He waited until the fourth wagon came alongside, then climbed up on to the tongue. Virginia Millais gave him a smile of welcome, moved along the seat. He took the reins from her, slapped the rumps of the horses absently.

'We're heading for the South Pass,' he said quietly, pointing towards the tall peaks which were now close on the horizon. 'Once we cross that and move down into the plains on the other side, it ought to be plain sailing all the way into California. I'm sure you'll all be glad once this journey is over.'

'And the border gangs you mentioned. What about them?'

'We may run into trouble with them.' His eyes followed those of the woman to the tall peaks that glistened in the sunlight. 'It's hard to say. But we fought off Jesse Sherman and his killers. I reckon we can do the same with these men.'

There was a movement in the wagon at Neil's back and a moment later the heavy folds of canvas were twitched aside. Neil felt his gaze being drawn to the golden-haired woman who looked out at him, her eyes turning to Virginia Millais and then back to him.

'They tell me that you're feeling a little better now, Ma'am,' said Neil quietly. 'I'm afraid I've never had the chance to talk with you, and thank you for saving my life as you did.'

There was an instant of pause, then: 'He was the man who gave the orders to stampede the cattle. He killed my husband just as surely as if he had trained a gun on him and pulled the trigger. He didn't deserve to live.'

'I'm real sorry about your husband.' Neil spoke hesitantly. 'He was a good man. It was a bad way for anyone to die.'

The woman's face did not change. Only her eye seemed alive. 'He's dead now, but life has to go on here whether we like it or not.'

'I understand. Perhaps when we reach California, it may be different. You may be able to start a new life there, pick up the threads and begin again.'

'Perhaps.' Her voice was merely a faint whisper of sound. Then it grew a little stronger. 'And you, Neil Roberts? What about you when we reach California? Do you intend to turn and ride back into this terrible country? Here, so they tell me, you're always on the run.'

'You seem to know a lot about me,' he said softly.

'Enough to know that you're no criminal, that the charges brought against you were made by crooked people, men who hid behind a badge and brought shame to this country.'

'I wish you could make everyone see that.' He spoke lightly, in a faintly bantering tone, but his words were deep and serious. His fingers had tightened a little, convulsively, on the leather reins in his hands.

'Then why don't you stay in California? Surely the past could never catch up with you there. It's new country, shut off from this place by the mountains. Like me, you're looking for some place to start a completely new life.' Her eyes looked over him with a renewed interest, as if seeing the man for the first time.

There was silence while the wagon lurched forward over the rough trail, the creak of the wheels loud in Neil's ears. It was a thought which had never occurred to him. Perhaps this woman was right. Perhaps in California, hundreds of miles from here, he might find the peace he had been seeking for so long and there would no longer be the need to keep on running, moving on from one place to another, with only the wide arch of the heaven for a ceiling, his saddle for a pillow.

'You'll consider it?' There was a trace of insistence in the woman's voice as she looked at him.

For an instant his gaze locked with hers, then he gave a slow, brief nod. 'I'll consider it,' he said softly. 'But first we have to reach California and that isn't going to be easy. We've still a long way to go and if there is snow up there in the Pass, it's going to be ten times worse than anything we've had to endure so far.'

The lie of the land was far rougher now than anything they had yet encountered. They forded a wide river, shallow, but with the current running fast. Already in flood, fed by the rains and snow up in the mountains, it boded ill for a crossing of the South Pass. Now they were moving into the foothills of the mountains. High above them, crushing down with all of their tremendous, massive weight, the mountains looked up against the bright blue of the sky, their topmost peaks almost lost to sight. Then the tall trees which covered the lower slopes crowded in on them from all sides, and although high noon blazed somewhere above the leafy arch over their heads, here it was blue-shadowed and still, with the air cool and filled with the sharply acrid scent of the pines.

Presently they came upon the relic of an ancient wagon trail, broader than that which they had followed from the plain, and they made good time with the horses pulling hard in the traces, the wagons rumbling forward, rocking gently from side to side. In places the trail wound around jagged rocks, then climbed to a long, bare ridge of stratum where they came out into the open, the trees thinning, then falling away from them on both sides so that the bright light of the glaring late-afternoon sun beat down at them with an intense fury that half-blinded them until their eyes became accustomed to it.

Halfway along the stratum they came across the remains of an old digging. There were two log cabins built by the side of the trail in the lee of a tall stretch of rock, but the roofs had fallen in and there was the mark of a solitary grave in the hard earth in front of a small clump of trees, the rough wooden cross thrusting itself up from the dirt like a vaguely accusing finger. Neil let his gaze wander over the scene, taking in everything until he was certain that the place was deserted and there was no danger there. In one of the trees an axe had been thrust into the bark, left there by the former occupant. At some time in the past, he thought, a man had driven that axe-head deep into the wood and then simply turned on his heel and walked away, possibly the man who had buried his companion in that lonely grave near the trees.

'Do you know this land, Neil?' Jackson turned from his seat on the lead wagon, holding the reins loosely in his huge gnarled hands.

'I've been here a couple of times before. There's a good place to camp about three miles ahead. We won't reach the pass for another three, four days maybe, depends on how fast we can travel.'

'You been all the way over and down to the other side?'

'I have, but not in the middle of winter. It may look easy right now, but when you're up there, in the middle of a blizzard, things look very different.'

By degrees the country roughened and, around them, the pines grew smaller, more stunted. They were climbing through the timber now, but the trail led them by many switchback courses, and Neil knew that the change would not be sudden, that only gradually would they notice the difference between the tree-covered slopes down here, where the air was still warm, particularly at high noon, and the rocky passes high up where the air was thin, and even if the sky was blue and cloudless, the air was cold and frosty; and the long nights filled with the bright and glittering stars were colder than any of these people had ever known.

They camped on the wide bluff some five hundred feet above the plain. There were crags and deep, knife-edged ravines all about them now and the wind that came sweeping down off the sheer side of the mountains was bitterly cold and struck through their clothing into their bones. The wagons were drawn up in single file and the two fires were lit in a shallow, narrow-sided ravine where they could not be picked out from the plains down below. Although Jesse Sherman was finished, there was still the possibility that Matt Hollard might come riding out on their heels, even though they had crossed his territory now.

They had held the wagons to the ridge during the latter part of the long afternoon, but now had dropped down into the ravines. Shortly before sunset they had crossed the narrow creek and there was plenty of fresh water for themselves and the horses. While the others ate their evening meal, cooked over the fires, Neil made his way to the edge of the bluff, checking on the ground. The land, he saw, was deceptive. They had passed out of one large canyon, up to this flat stretch of ground, and in front of them stretched another canyon, although the trail itself was still pointed at the summit of the mountains. Now they were on an island of height with a sheer precipitous drop of three hundred feet on one side of the trail directly ahead of them. He peered along it in the growing darkness, trying to make out details. It would not be easy to drive along that particular stretch of the trail, he estimated, and there was a very narrow trail running down the side of the precipice, a trail which could have been traversed only by a mule or a mountain goat. Certainly nothing else could have been sufficiently surefooted to make it and he could see that this trail had not been used for a long time. Possibly it could not have been anything more than a series of footholds cut out by goats.

The cliff itself was rock and earth, growing a stunted kind of vegetation which clung tenaciously to it, sucking a bare existence from the dry soil with the solid rock only an inch or so beneath. The darkness fell swiftly as he stood there and the night air began to flow more swiftly off the peaks, sweeping down the narrow ravines. He shivered and made his way slowly back to the camp. Clem Jackson motioned him down beside the fire, his eyes drifting slowly around the looming rocks which lay about them at the shadows that crouched beyond the ring of red light thrown by the leaping flames. A platter of sizzling beef was placed in front of

Neil, and the other waited until the platter was clean before saying quietly: 'What do you think of it? You did go to take a look along the trail?'

'We'll have to be careful when we pull out in the morning. There's a sheer drop of nearly three hundred feet on one side. One false move and that wagon will be finished.' He forced a quick smile, but there was no answering smile from Clem Jackson. The big man gnawed at his dry lips.

'There's no sign of snow,' he said finally, the words deep rumbling things that came from the depths of his chest.

'The weather can be deceptive here. It can change without warning.'

Jackson shrugged, gulped his coffee. Jessup refilled his cup and the big man held the cup between his hands, rolling it a little, absorbing the heat, then held the coffee beneath his broad nose, sniffing the fragrance and drawing it deep into his lungs.

'How soon before we hit the bad country, Neil?'

'Maybe three days. The trail winds around the outcrops of rock most of the way now. We'll have to move the wagons one at a time past the precipice. Once we're beyond that, we ought to make better time, although it's going to be uphill all the way now.'

Neil filled his coffee cup from the boiler and sipped it slowly, swilling it around his mouth before swallowing it. It brought some of the warmth back into his frozen body.

Later, getting up from the fire, he made his way back along the line of wagons. They stood in shadow now that the light had gone from the sky, but as he moved quietly past one of them there was a slight movement of the canvas and a voice came out of the darkness, a rich and husky voice that he recognised immediately.

'Neil...' called Claire Vance. 'Neil, do you mind if I talk to you?'

8

The White Menace

Bending forward a little, Neil stared up at the questioning eyes of the woman who looked down at him from the tongue of the wagon. She drew her shawl more tightly about her shoulders in the cold night air.

Then her hand reached out and she placed it on his arm.

'Do you mind if I talk to you, Neil?'

'No.'

He felt a curious tightness in his body as if his muscles were all drawing tight under his flesh. It was easy to forget Sherman and Hollard, to forget the life he had been forced to lead in the past, for ever running from the law, sleeping where he could, never knowing how long it would be before some gun, faster than his own, caught up with him and ended his life in a single, red-edged instant of time. He sensed her nearness and felt the strange warmth that seemed to flow from her hand into his arm, even through the thick cloth.

'Did you think over what I told you some days back, Neil?'

'About settling down in California, if we ever get there?'

'Yes.'

'I've thought about it a little.' He straightened up as she sank down on to the hard wood of the wagon, sat beside him, staring up at the brilliant stars that powdered the heavens over their heads, frostily clear now. Soon, thought Neil tightly, those stars would be even clearer until the time came when they were utterly blotted out by the racing snow clouds.

'And you don't like the idea. Is that it?' Her voice was soft and low. There was no trace in her voice or face of the trouble that she had experienced on the drive, the loss of her husband and the time when she had shot a man in the back.

'I think it may be a good idea. But I wonder if a man like me could ever settle down and try to forget the past, or whether it wouldn't keep on coming up, standing between me and any peace I might find.'

'It wouldn't if you were determined to forget it. If you only wanted to put it behind you and kept it there.' She paused, then tightened her grip on his arm. 'If you want something hard enough, nothing in this world will stop you.'

'I only wish I had your kind of faith, Claire,' he said softly.

She leaned to one side. Her shoulder touched his and her weight rested on his arm. 'Do you know that's the first time you've ever spoken my name.'

'I never realised.'

'I hope you do decide to settle down there, and not come riding back to look for vengeance.'

'Why should you think I'm seeking vengeance now?'

'I'm not sure. I know how things were between you and that man I had to shoot. There was some kind of personal feud between you that could only be settled when one of you was dead. Now he's gone, but there are others back there who would like to see you dead, aren't there?'

He hesitated, knew that he could never lie to this woman, that she saw things about men more clearly than they realised. 'Yes, there are men here who won't rest until they've killed me. But Sherman was the worst. He was the last of the gang who framed me all those years ago.'

'And yet you're still running? Why?'

'Because the wanted notices are still out for me. Because decent lawmen believed the lies they spread around, believed them enough to put a price on my head. What chance do you reckon I'd have if I gave myself up and tried to prove that I was innocent of everything?'

'I think I understand. But California is a new country, a whole new world just over the top of those mountains. There are no crooked sheriffs there who know the name of Neil Roberts. And there aren't likely to be any riding out there looking for you – no bounty hunters coming as far afield as that.'

'I wish I could be sure of that.'

'When we get there – and I'm sure we'll get there one day, I hope you will be sure. You and I are very much alike, Neil. We both seem to be looking for the same thing, and this new country that lies ahead of us is the last and only chance we'll ever get. We both want peace, peace to forget everything that has happened and start with a clean sheet. It isn't going to be easy for a woman without a man out there. This is a world that men have made, and there's no place in it for a woman like me, not unless she wants to go up into the hills and shut herself away in some small hut where nobody can ever find her, or she goes the other way, becomes a bad woman.'

'You'll never be like that,' he said fervently.

'Someday I will. But before that happens there are so many things I want.'

Neil shivered, threw a swift glance at the clear arch of the sky about him. Already he thought he detected the touch of snow on the breath of the wind.

Carefully, one behind the other, the wagons edged forward along the trail. The men sat gingerly on the tongues of the wagons, guiding the horses slowly while the women and children walked behind along the stony trail. In places the earth had formed a fresh slide across the trail, dirt not yet packed firm. There was no point in risking the lives of everyone, and Neil noticed the eyes of the women and children flicking incessantly towards the bottom of the canyon down below them less than three feet from where they walked, but three hundred feet down. There was water at the bottom, silver and thread-like, made narrow by distance.

One by one the wagons negotiated the precarious section of the trail. The women and the children climbed back on board, and they swung forward along the winding trail, heading up into the upper fastnesses of the mountains. The air grew thinner as they moved higher, thinner and colder. There were more narrow creeks to be crossed, high banks with loose rocks that moved whenever the wheels of the wagons crushed over them. Water foamed white over the boulders, splashed over the axles of the wagons as they crossed. Slowly the weather and the terrain was building up a picture of what lay in store for them, and Neil found the apprehension in his mind growing with every mile they travelled. Above them the towering peaks still lifted, high and seemingly inaccessible. It seemed incredible that they could ever get the wagons up there and, in places, the trail narrowed until it was all they could do to move the Conestogas through between the rough, rocky walls of the rearing canyons through which they had to pass.

Two days, three, and then on the fourth day there was no sun at first light. The dawn was a vague greyness that spread up from below them, touched the sky with a curious eerie light. Rolling out of his blankets, feeling the cold dampness on his body, Neil glanced up at the clouds that moved in swiftly from the north-east, blowing over the ragged peaks, and knew that there was snow on the way, that the luck which had been with them for so long had given out.

He folded his blanket, then moved over to the embers of the night's fire, kicked them with the toe of his boot until it broke flame, and piled more dry wood on to it until the flames leapt high and the boiler of coffee was sizzling over it. The others rolled out of their blankets, shrugged, and then stood up. Jackson rubbed the sleep from his eyes, then stared about him, caught Neil's worried look and walked over, stood with his hands outstretched towards the fire.

'Think it spells trouble, Neil?'

'Afraid so. Those clouds mean snow. We ought to reach this end of the pass by noon. Could be that we can be well into it before the snow comes. But there'll be a blizzard before night.'

'I figure you're right. What do you say to that, Jessup?'

The other nodded, pursed his lips tightly. 'This is country I don't know, Jackson. But I'll take your word for it. Want me to get the train moving as soon as possible?'

Jackson nodded. Soon there was the smell of sizzling beef and bacon, with beans scooped on to the platters. Breakfast was a hurried meal of silences, soon over. Then the train pulled out once more, moving through a country of almost unsurpassed grandeur; a beautiful terrain, a magnificent vista which seemed to defy the imagination. But in spite of its beauty, it could be capricious and deadly.

The people in the wagons stared about them with open eyes. This was something none of them had ever seen before, something new and strange. By noon, with the clouds still lowering over the crests of the mountains, they had reached the eastern end of the South Pass. In front of them the ground stretched for mile upon mile, almost level with the tall, towering rocks lifting sheer on either side of them, a vast natural cutting that stretched clear over the mountain chain. Soon there was no talk in the wagons. The first few white flakes drifted down in the wind.

Twenty minutes later the blizzard struck, a million white flakes that swirled about the wagons, obliterating the rocky walls on either side. Men rode with their heads down, shivering in their thick clothing. The snow worked its way down their necks in spite of the high collars and wide-brimmed hats, into their boots. The blast of the wind, seeping along the pass, threatened to hurl them back into the rocks, and the animals made little headway against it.

This was worse than Neil had expected. He had hoped that they would have made it halfway along the Pass before the blizzard struck. Another blast of chill air lashed at them, this time off the walls of the pass, hit so hard that the horses were forced to stop in their tracks and brace themselves against it, unable to move. Neil cursed harshly under his breath, lifted his head a little and tried to peer into the heart of the snowstorm. Already it was beginning to settle around them, forming a white layer on the uneven ground, even beginning to stick to the rocky walls of the canyon.

It made an even greater danger now, obliterating the rocks and boulders in the middle of the trail so that they could not pick them out in time, before the wheels ran over them, sending the wagons lurching and swaying from side to side. There was one thing, he thought quickly, if there was anyone following them it would blot out their trail completely.

'Do you think we can keep going in this?' shouted Jackson at the top of his voice. He bent from the wagon as Neil rode alongside. His body was almost covered in snow, his face covered by the hood which he had pulled down over his eyes so that only the shaggy beard showed, thrust forward aggressively.

'We've got to. It won't let up for days, possibly weeks. I know these blizzards. Once they begin, they just keep on going.'

Heads down, they pushed ahead into the storm. Everything was a solid wall of white and it was impossible to see more than three feet in any direction. Overhead, the sky was a deep and ominous grey, with no let-up in the icy wind. Minutes stretched themselves into hours as the numbing cold bit deep into their bodies. Even inside the wagons there was no escape from the driving snow. It worked its way through the folds of the canvas, formed a deep layer on the tops of the wagons, threatened to tear the canvas. The horses trudged forward, heads down, moving by some strange instinct.

How they managed to survive the biting fingers of the wind, the driving snow which was piling high on all sides, it was impossible to tell. When night came it did not bring an end to their misery. Rather it was just beginning.

Jessup tried to build a fire in the lee of the rock, with the snow shrieking past, but it was virtually impossible. They huddled close to the flames and tried to get some warmth into their frozen bodies. Savagely the wind howled around them, threatening to tear the heavy canvas from the wagons, exposing their interiors.

'If we ever get through this, meeting up with those border gangs is going to be child's play,' growled Jessup tightly. He rubbed the snow from his face and eyes, shook his head numbly. 'I don't mind facing up to something I can see and fight, but how in God's name can you fight this?'

'You can't,' Neil told him, pushing his hands out towards the flames. You've got to accept it, try to go with it. Just tell yourself it would be even worse if we'd taken Snake Pass. If it doesn't get too deep, we ought to be all right. But if the Pass gets blocked before we make our way through it, then I reckon those of you who know how to pray had better start, because we'll need all the luck we can get. There's no turning back now. We've committed ourselves to getting through, and if it means fighting this every hour of the day and night, then that's how it's got to be. Better get that into your minds right away.'

He turned his head slowly, looked at one man after the other, trying to read the expression on their faces. There was a little fear there, he saw, a little apprehension, but at the moment it was all hidden under the terrible surface numbness that came from the constant battering by that icy wind and the driving clouds of snow.

Jackson got heavily to his feet, moved over to the cook-pot, pulled out a long strip of beef and thrust it between his teeth. With an equal slowness, he filled his cup with coffee and drank it down, then returned to his place beside Neil.

Calder, thin-faced and short, pushed his legs towards the fire, said harshly: 'I've got the feelin' that we're making a drive we'll never finish. No one told us that it would be anything like this. We'll never ride out this blizzard. We ought to have waited down in the plain until the winter passed.'

'Don't you realise it yet? We didn't have enough supplies to do that.' Neil spoke more sharply than he had intended. 'We'd all have starved to death before the winter was through. And there's another thing. There was the chance that Matt Hollard might be riding out on our trial, coming to finish what Sherman started out to do.'

Calder shook his head in a bird-like fashion. 'You've been scaring us with this talk about Hollard all the way here, Roberts. I don't believe most of it for one. Seems you may have some idea in your mind that by coming with this train you'll be safe from the law, which I understand is still on your trail. If you'd been forced to stay back there, they'd have come riding after you and then you'd have been taken back to Dodge or Abilene to stand trial. What was it they accused you of, Roberts? Murder, wasn't it? They say you shot down a couple of men in the street.'

By a supreme effort of will, Neil held in his surging anger. Keeping his voice lightly controlled and even, he said through clenched teeth: 'That ain't quite true, and I reckon you know it, Calder. Sure I killed some men a few years back, but they were crooked lawmen who would have shot me down without just cause. But the sheriff managed to get my name put out on the wanted circulars throughout the territory, and nobody seemed to inquire whether or not there was any truth or justification for it.'

'Seems we only got your word for that. You seemed mighty anxious to lead this train all the way through to California. I ain't denying that you seem to know this country, but I'm beginning to wonder why you came along. I ain't forgetting either that we've lost some good folk because of the fight between you and the cattle bosses here.'

'They would have killed us all if they had been able to,' interrupted Jessup harshly, turning on the other. 'We needed somebody with a fast gun who wouldn't be afraid to stand up to them.'

'Seems we really got somebody like that,' muttered Calder hoarsely.

'I'd hate to think of what might have happened to us if we hadn't,' said Jackson quickly. He turned and glared at the other, forcing him to a sullen silence. The logs crackled on the fire and there was an occasional hiss as the snowflakes whirled around the corner of the rocks and fell into the flames.

At first light the next morning they began to move out again. Tired men and tired horses. The snow lay more thickly about them now, almost two feet in depth, and was still falling, although the wind was no longer as strong or as blustery as on the previous day, but the snow still fell as thickly as before, and there were no breaks in the clouds, no sign of the sun.

For most of the day they travelled without mishap. Then, during the afternoon, they reached a spot where the ground became more open, the rocky walls which had hemmed them in all the way were no longer so close. In front of them the floor of the pass stretched in an unbroken sheet of white, the snow smooth and unsullied.

At the head of the train Neil reined his mount and lifted his right hand to halt the train. Slowly, reluctantly, the wagons ground to a standstill.

'What's wrong, Neil?' boomed Jackson, from his perch on the lead wagon.

'I'm not sure. Just a feeling, I guess.'

The other peered ahead through the thickly falling snow, staring out under thick brows, covered now with snow. 'I don't see anything wrong. Looks all right to me.'

'Maybe so. But there may be danger up ahead. In country like this there may be chasms splitting across the floor of the pass, and it only needs a horse to put his foot into one of them and we lose not only the horse but the wagon as well.'

'What do you suggest then?'

'You'd better stay here. I'll ride on ahead and take a good look-see. If there is any danger there, the sooner we know about it, the better.'

He gigged his sorrel. The animal moved forward slowly and carefully, picking its own pace. The horse was both tired and doubtful, seemed to sense that there was something wrong, increasing the feeling of apprehension in Neil's mind. The stud frequently stopped and had to be prodded forward before it would take another step. Turning in the saddle after a few minutes of this slow progress, Neil felt a momentary twinge of surprise, realising that he could no longer see the train, that it had been blotted out completely by the curtain of snow.

He could not have travelled more than twenty yards, and yet there was neither sight nor sound of the train. The snow utterly muffled any sound and he had the impression of being utterly and completely isolated, cut off, in a nightmare world of white.

On his left the edge of the trail suddenly pitched downwards into a deep canyon whose bottom he could not see. The sorrel gathered its feet closely together and began to mince a little, hesitant, winding itself around and around, trying to reverse its direction, until it was facing the way back to the wagons. Holding tightly to the reins, Neil forced it to turn and begin moving forward once more. They had gone less than fifty yards when the sorrel halted once more, stuck in its feet and refused to budge, no matter how he coaxed it. Slowly he slid from the saddle, moved forward gingerly on foot, placing one foot in front of the other, feeling his way forward, confident now that there was some kind of danger here, danger which he could not see as yet.

Then his left foot went from under him, slid away as there was no trail to meet him.

Losing his balance, he toppled forward into sheer emptiness. Only the fact that he was still holding on to the leather of the reins and that the sorrel had dug in its feet saved him at that moment. Swiftly, with a savage instinct, his hand tightened on the reins and he felt himself jerked upward as the sorrel pulled up its head in alarm. For a long moment he hung there, suspended in mid-air, feet swinging loosely under him, unable to obtain a grip or foothold. His other foot had slipped off the trail the moment he had lost his balance. Somehow he managed to prevent himself from panicking, maintained his hold on the reins and slowly swung his body back towards the trail, holding his breath in his lungs until it hurt, praying that the sorrel would not move forward or they would both go crashing to their deaths in the chasm that yawned below them.

Slowly, speaking gently to the sorrel, he managed to swing his legs back on to the trail, sought for and found a precarious hold, dug in his toes and hung there, scarcely daring to breathe. Then, inch by inch, the sorrel moved back, away from the slippery edge, on to the firm ground of the trail.

Neil found lodgement for his feet, heaved

backward and managed to stand up straight, slowly placing his weight on the rock. It was covered with ice under the snow, but there were a couple of upthrusting rocks, and somehow he succeeded in wedging his feet into them, fighting to maintain his uneasy balance. He walked back to the break in the trail, shuffling his feet now until he reached it, and knew himself to be on firm ground. Then he swung himself up into the saddle and urged the sorrel back to the waiting train.

'There's a slide back there,' he said brusquely to Jackson. 'Sheer drop into the chasm down on the left. Trail's broken there and we'll have to move around it before we can be sure we're safe. It ain't going to be easy, but unless we do, we're stuck here for good. Better pass the word along to the others. Then we'll move out. We've wasted too much time as it is.'

He rode back along the whole length of the train, giving his orders to the others. They listened in silence, their faces almost completely hidden by the broad hoods pulled down over their eyes, the hands muffled in thick gloves. He knew how they must have been feeling at that moment, bodies numbed and frozen, with scarcely

241

any sensation in their hands and feet. Yet they had to be made to move on, into the teeth of that howling blizzard, along the trail where danger lurked at every turn, and to fall out of the train meant certain death for the people in any stranded wagon. There were many tales in this part of the west concerning wagon trains that had moved out over the mountains and had never been heard of again, had certainly never reached their destination. Whether they had perished up here in the wild passes or had been set upon by the border gangs and totally destroyed, the wagons looted of all their possessions and then burned by the gunslammers, no one knew.

At last they were ready to pull out and Neil led the way, moving close to the wagons, urging them to keep together, not to lose sight of the one in front. Ten yards in that swirling blizzard, tens of millions of white flakes streaming across one's vision and everything was lost behind that curtain of white.

Coming to the break in the trail, Neil paused, pushed himself upright in the saddle, then signalled to Jackson to move forward slowly, to swing away to the right, away from the edge where the rock fell away into nothingness, down into the stretching depths of the chasm that loomed on that edge of the trail. Had it not been for that strange sixth sense of his, something he had never been able to explain, but which had saved him so many times in the past that he had learned never to ignore it, they might have all gone plunging over the side into oblivion.

It was a dangerous, tricky business getting those wagons past the break in the trail. Neil had expected no trouble with Jackson, nor with Jessup. Both men knew how to handle horses, even when the animals, sensing danger, threatened to rear and panic away from the spot. But there were others in the wagons who did not have that experience, and Neil was forced to station himself on the very lip of that steep drop and allow the wagons to move past him. It only needed one of the horses to bolt and he would be finished, thrust off the trail by the panicking animal, knocked to one side by the careering weight and bulk of the wagon.

Then, after what seemed an interminable period, they were all past, moving on slowly into the swirling snowstorm, canvas tops swaying from side to side, but more slowly now with all that weight of snow lying on top of them.

Another camp that night with the cold dampness seeping into their bones. There was the misery of not being dry, of wet clothing clinging to their bodies, irritating and chafing at the flesh until it had been torn and opened by the roughness of their garments.

There was little wood here to light a fire, and once it went out during the later part of the night, the cold became more intense than anything they had ever known before.

Neil considered that up here in the pass itself there would be no danger from outlaw bands, or even from Hollard if he was following them, and he knew that it would be both dangerous and unnecessary to post guards to keep a look out for trouble. The men needed all the sleep they could get, and it seemed wrong to deny them it just because of the million-to-one chance that gunhawks might come upon them in the middle of the blizzard.

Progress was measured in yards most of the way. If they succeeded in travelling half a mile a day, they considered themselves to be making good progress. Primitive and raw, nature fought them with everything at her disposal, as if to show them how puny they really were, that if she wished she could destroy them utterly.

There were cold mornings and colder nights, men clustered around the fires when they had the chance, and now the stops along the trail were becoming more and more frequent as the men grew more tired and the horses needed the rests.

There seemed to be no end to the pass, or the snow. It swirled around them as they rode with their bodies hunched forward over the reins or the necks of their mounts, eyes and nostrils clogged by the beating snow. It seemed incredible that these small, feathery flakes could do so much damage, could be so devastating.

The folk with the train began to murmur among themselves, but although he knew of this Neil did not consider it dangerous. They had long since passed the point of no return, now they had to go on because to turn back would mean certain death.

Then, two weeks after they had entered the pass, the snowstorm abated. Now they were fighting their way through deep drifts which, in places, threatened to engulf the wagons themselves, although fortunately the sheer walls of the pass had shielded most of the trail from the full fury of the storm. The sky cleared, the dark, lowering clouds blew away and, with the sudden change in the weather, they discovered that they were no longer moving level, but were descending down the further levels of the mountains.

They had moved through them, had weathered one of the worst blizzards in the South Pass, and were now dipping down towards the stretching, fertile plains that lay beyond.

Less than a hundred miles to the west lay the frontier with California. As if anxious to reach there, the men pushed their wagons to the limit now. The coming of the clear weather, even though the air was still cold, had brought a new life to the folk in the train. There was the feeling that they had surmounted every possible difficulty, that nothing could now prevent them from getting through, that they were safe from all trouble and danger.

Perhaps it was this which almost proved to be their undoing. Reaching the level plains, they moved on in a cloud of their own dust, still heading west, not once deviating from the trail.

They had come across almost a thousand miles of some of the worst country in the whole of the United States, had forged a trail across the continent which would prove to be the beginning of the tremendous movement to the west, would lead to the eventual population of the State of California.

There was laughter now among the wagons, laughter that seemed to ease the strain of the past few months when everything had seemed to be conspiring against them to prevent them from reaching their destination. Now they were in sight of it, and they felt certain that nothing more could go wrong, that if there were any more dangers, they could not be as bad as those they had already faced on the way, and they could meet them and overcome them easily.

Inside, Neil did not share their optimism. True, they had fought off the hired killers of the cattle barons to the east, they had met and forded rivers swollen in flood, and they had crossed the South Pass through a tremendous blizzard when it had seemed that nothing could possibly survive.

Now, in front of them, stretching for mile upon endless mile, as far as the eye could see, reaching out to the flat, distant horizons to the west, lay the great plains.

Riding ahead of the train, Neil turned in

his saddle, feeling the sun warm on his head and shoulders, the dust on his face and cracked lips, getting under his eyes, blurring his vision. But anything seemed better than the snow up there in the pass. Behind him, stretched out over two miles of the prairie, the wagons were strung out in single file, rumbling forward.

But, looking at them, it was hard to realise that these were the same wagons that had set out from the eastern boundary of Jesse Sherman's territory all those long weary weeks before. Then they had been brightly painted, with white canvas stretched over the backs. Now that canvas was torn and shredded by the tearing fingers of the winds up there in the mountains and the soaking it had received during their crossing of the great rivers to the east. The paintwork was scratched and scoured, and the men who drove those wagons were all changed too. Now they were lean, gaunt men with deep-set eyes, brighter than before, eyes that had looked out upon the far horizons and witnessed the great open spaces of prairie and mountain. Men with wide hats and long-barrelled Winchesters thrust into the scabbards by their sides.

On the third night, with the wagons in a

wide circle, the fires lit in the centre, the stock herded there for safety, with two look-outs moving slowly around the outer perimeter, Neil rolled himself into his blankets near one of the wagons, listening to the occasional crackle of the fire and the faint sound of the wind sighing over the prairie. In the distance he could just hear the low, mournful voices of the guards as they sang the songs of the Deep South, to keep up their spirits and to keep themselves awake until the others came to relieve them.

Another five days on the trail, he thought inwardly, and they would have reached their destination, and then his work would be done.

He would have finished what he had set out to do, would have fulfilled his promise to take this wagon train to California.

And then what of him, what of Neil Roberts, wanted in Idaho and Arkansas for murder, even though it had been the murder of a crooked sheriff?

He turned over Claire Vance's words in his mind, considering them seriously for the first time. Before he had merely allowed them to pass through his brain without really concentrating on them.

Now he held fast to them, turned them

over and over in his thoughts. It was possible that, in California, he might be able to settle down and put the past behind him, never think of it again. Then, as he lay there, he found his thoughts slipping away to Claire Vance herself. The memory of her nearness that night, the feel of her slim hand on his arm, was still strong within him, and he doubted if he would ever forget that.

For a moment he pondered on the memory of the tall, golden-haired woman, then all thought of her, all thought of California and what might happen there, was driven from his mind. The sharp bark of gunfire came from the near distance, and close on its heels, he heard the drumming of running horses coming nearer.

Swiftly he was on his feet, the blanket thrown on one side, the Colts whispering into his hands as he came upright and turned to face the sound.

The two guards were firing into the darkness, loosing off shot after shot. A few moments later they moved back out of the shadows, and came into the ring of the wagons.

'What is it?' demanded Jackson, running forward, his huge face alight.

'Gunhawks!' muttered one of the men.

His right arm hung limp by his side. He held the Winchester in the other, turned and pointed. More gunfire broke out and then Neil made out the horses as they came plunging forward out of the darkness.

Bullets hummed and droned through the air close to his body as he flung himself forward, hitting the ground behind one of the wheels of the nearest wagon. He fired swiftly at the fleeting shadows, saw a man topple from the saddle, one leg caught in the stirrup, his mount dragging him over the rough ground.

More vivid flashes in the starlit darkness, more riders converging on the wagon train. One of the riders put his horse to the shafts of a wagon, leapt over them into the centre of the ring.

Turning, without pausing to take a deliberate aim, Neil fired. The first shot missed its target. The second took the man in the shoulder, slamming him sideways in the saddle.

Rifles opened up from the wagons. The whole of the train was awake now. Everyone was a gunman now – a fighter. The women were firing and loading. Harsh voices yelled as the gunhawks were met by a hail of fire that poured into their ranks, thinning them savagely.

More yells from the darkness around the camp. Now there were more bullets flying through the air, hammering off the metal uprights of the wagons, shrieking thinly in distorted ricochet.

Neil felt something pluck at his left shoulder, winced involuntarily. How long could the firing last? Half an hour? An hour perhaps? It was impossible to tell, for when a man's life depended on killing his enemy first before he was killed himself, no one thought of time.

'They're turning away,' yelled Jessup, shouting the words at the top of his voice. Neil lifted his head, peering into the dimness, saw that what the other said was true. There were unmoving shadows on the ground around the perimeter of the camp now. It had been a grim and cold business. There had been no quarter asked and none given. California lay only a few miles distant, and nothing was going to stop these people from getting there. They had been through too much for that to happen.

For the rest of the night Neil remained awake, eyes watching the darkness, but there were no further attacks, and in the morning they bandaged up the wounds of the men who had been hit, ate a meal of jerked beef, washed down with weak coffee, and moved along the trail again.

Ten nights later they made camp beside a wide river that flowed sluggishly between low banks, the water muddy from the recent rains, but the current slow and leisurely.

With the sunrise, they crossed the river, the Conestoga wagons rumbling slowly on to the broad strip of ground that lay beyond, over into the State of California, into a bright and golden sunrise that sent light flooding over the whole stretch of territory around them. For the first time since they had left the East, even Neil felt that the danger was past for them. Slowly he reined his mount, and watched as the wagons rolled by, slowly, cumbersome and heavy. But they were bringing a new state into being. These were the pioneers, he thought, with a sudden sense of pride. These were the men and women who had not been daunted by the dangers which had faced them along the thousand miles they had crossed. They had brought with them some vital spark which was so necessary if this part of the continent was now going to live and become ready to take its place with the others in the years that were to come.

He sat tall and straight in the saddle, on a

small knoll, shading his eyes against the sunlight. Was it his imagination, or was the air here really warmer and gentler than back east? He shrugged, then turned his head.

Already the wagon train was beginning to pull away from him. Slowly, he raked spurs over the flanks of the sorrel, turned his back on the mountains to the east, keeping the sunrise at his back, and rode to where a tall, golden-haired woman waved to him from one of the wagons.

The publishers hope that this book has given you enjoyable reading. Large Print Books are especially designed to be as easy to see and hold as possible. If you wish a complete list of our books please ask at your local library or write directly to:

Dales Large Print Books
Magna House, Long Preston,
Skipton, North Yorkshire.
BD23 4ND

FIRE

LEED

ANIKAL BRUV

KITCHEN DRAWER

BEET ROOTS